ANATOMIES

A|P

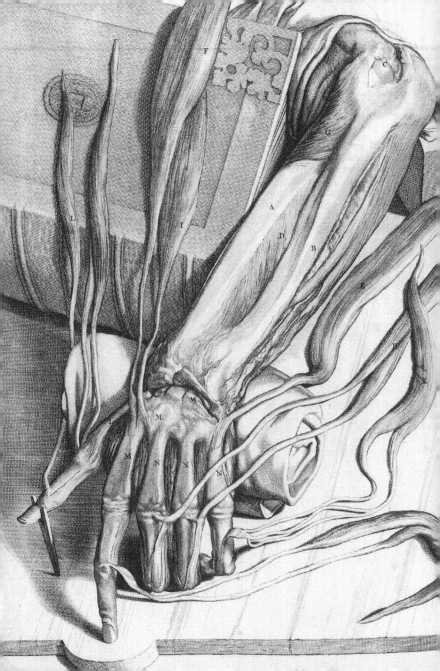

ANATOMIES

SUSAN MCCARTY

AFOREMENTIONED PRODUCTIONS

A|P

Published by Aforementioned Productions. Aforementioned and AP colophon are trademarks of Aforementioned Productions, Inc.

Stories in this collection originally appeared, some in varied form, in the following journals: "Kindness" in *Barrelhouse*, "Fellowship" in *Willow Springs*, "Full" in *The Los Angeles Review*, "Another Zombie Story" in *Indiana Review*, "The Last Night They Spent Together before the Separation" in *Wigleaf*, "Anatomies" originally appeared as "City/Body: Fragments" in *Conjunctions*, "Pest" in *Everyday Genius*, "Field Reports" in *The Collagist*, "Like Acrobats" originally appeared as "The Lost One" in *West Branch*, "Indirect Object" in *apt*, "Corridors" in *Gargoyle*, "Shearing Day" in *Flyway*, "Between the Land and the Sky" in *Denver Quarterly*, "The Fat of the Land" in *Connu*, "Homework" in *Northwest Review*, and "Anamnesis" in *Tarpaulin Sky*.

ISBN 978-1-941143-03-2

Published June 2015

Cover design by Carissa Halston

Cover illustrations by Joseph Maclise for *The anatomy of the arteries of the human body, with its applications to pathology and operative surgery* (London, 1844).

Book design by Carissa Halston

Interior illustrations by Gérard de Lairesse, and engraved by Abraham Blooteling and Peter van Gunst, for *Ontleding des menschelyken lichaams* (Amsterdam, 1690).

Printed in the United States of America

aforementioned.org

For Jenny and Marshall.

[DIS]SECTIONS

ANIMALIA

Anatomies	1
Fellowship	19
Indirect Object	47
Kindness	69
The Fat of the Land	97

HISTOLOGY

Pest	117
Full	118
Corridors	120
Passive-Aggressive	122
The Last Night They Spent Together before the Separation	124
Between the Land and the Sky	129

BACTERIUM

Field Reports	135
Another Zombie Story	153
The Good Son	165
Shearing Day	183
Like Acrobats	203
Homework	215

Anamnesis: An Epilogue	241

The love story...is the tribute the lover must pay to the world in order to be reconciled with it.

— Roland Barthes, *A Lover's Discourse*

Certain themes are incurable.

— Lyn Hejinian, *The Language of Inquiry*

ANIMALIA

{the taxonomic kingdom comprising all animals (including human beings)}

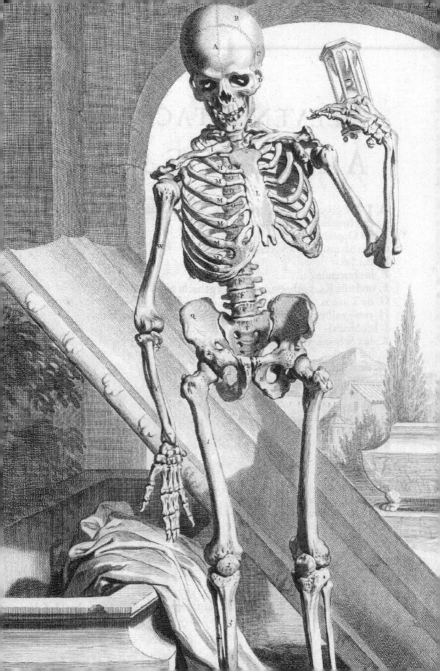

ANATOMIES

Corner of A and Fourth/Eye

In New York, there is an important distinction to make between where you live and where you sleep. You sleep in your apartment. You live in the city.

It is a dripping August, which you know by the smell of it: dried urine, rotting garbage, and the unleaded smell of cabs burning off fuel as they idle in the shimmering heat, each a mirage, a promise of something better on the other side. You can't get into a cab today because the ten dollars in cash and change sitting on your desk in your apartment is all you have until payday, which is Friday. Today is Sunday. You don't have a bank account because the check-cashing place is convenient to your apartment. Also, you don't trust yourself with a bank account; the margin of error is always, always so small. Instead, you like to watch the stack of cash dwindle in front of you. It causes you anxiety, but it also makes you feel as though you are in control of something here, in New York. You are in control of nothing, of course, but the illusion helps.

Because you sleep in the East Village, in a studio apartment in an old tenement that you share with a roommate, you walk the streets for entertainment. On paydays, you allow yourself a Cuban sandwich from the takeout counter on Avenue A. Today, however, you simply stand in front of the door for a few minutes, because smelling something is almost as good as eating it, and smelling something other than urine and garbage makes you happy. The smells are engrossing, in fact, which is why you don't notice what has been going on behind you until there is the sound of something whining through the air, not very far from your head, and then the noise of the bystanders, who must have been there all along, suddenly rushes in and you turn in time to see two men grappling with each other, in the street, just feet away. One of them has a hammer. In the moment it has taken you to notice the scene and become confused by it, the man with the hammer bounces it off the side of the other man's head and there is a sound that would, under other circumstances, be satisfying—the sound of a job being completed, of something being forced into its proper place. You actually see the eye of the struck man wobble in its socket, as if it has just been dropped there to settle. They are both screaming—one in anger and the other in pain—but the sidewalkers are screaming too and so the scene takes on a kind of miserable white noise wherein no one person's distress can be sorted from another's.

The police sirens are what finally cut through the cord that had knotted around you, anchoring you to this place to watch a man maybe get killed. This is true for everyone, and when the cop car screeches up, the men have already run off together, wild elopers, one with his hand over his eye and a trail of blood down his shirt, the other just behind him, brandishing the hammer like a cartoon wife with a rolling pin after a mouse.

St. Vincent's/Lower Left Quadrant

David Beckham has broken the second metatarsal of his left foot. You do not care very much except that the picture of him in the sporting publication open on your lap—he sits on the ground, one hand over an eye, one hand on the foot, worried and in pain—is the only thing distracting you from your own pain (back, lower left quadrant), which is unlike any pain you've had before. It is also distracting you from the St. Vincent's ER, which is the least comforting place you've ever been. Everything is a shade of grayish green. There are no plants or tissue boxes. There are spots of dried blood on the floor in front of you. You sit facing the windows and feel

3

like you're in prison. You are trying not to pay attention to the couple seated to your left. You try to focus instead on the lesser pain of Becks, but your neighbors are difficult not to overhear.

It's the meth, the boyfriend says, he's been doing it all weekend. The ER attendant asks the man who is not the boyfriend how much meth he has done this weekend. The man is weeping quietly. He sits straight up in the green vinyl chair, one hand gripping the chair arm, the other twisting his boyfriend's hand, which has gone white and slightly blue from the pressure. His eyes don't look anywhere. I don't know, all of it? says the boyfriend, grimacing at his twisted hand, but content to bruise, to share. The expressionless attendant makes a note on a clipboard. And when did he do the, uh, procedure? she asks. I don't know, says the boyfriend. I just woke up and went to the bathroom and he was sitting on the toilet like that. Like what? asks the attendant just because she wants to hear it again. With his...the boyfriend whispers but can't talk too quietly because his man has started to make a low whining sound in his throat. With his testicles stapled to his thigh, he finishes and puts a hand on the head of the whining man who is wearing loose, dry-weave exercise shorts.

You have glanced up from Becks to catch this glimpse

4

and you'd almost forgotten yourself but here is the breathless punch again. You jerk in your seat and pant. Your vision tunnels, momentarily, the periphery dark and fogged out. You seem to pulse in empathy with your neighbor. Later, you will learn that a UTI has crawled up your urinary tract to your kidneys, which are infected. This can be life threatening but is also easily treatable.

The man with the staples in his balls lets out a thin howl, which is unlike a dog howl. It is not rounded and full and conclusive. It's the sound of pure pain. The ER attendant has come back out of the triage station and even she looks concerned now. You look back down at the photo because you feel very strongly that you would also like to howl, that you would like to hold this man's hand and go a little hysterical with him.

There is a bustling—the attendant and the boyfriend are trying to coax the patient into a wheelchair. You can't imagine how he got here, how he walked at all, down the stairs of his apartment building, to the curb to hail a cab. It must have taken tremendous reserves of strength. He must be exhausted. There is a yelp and a moan followed by some rustling, and the squeak of rubber tires on sanitized linoleum.

David Beckham looks very tired and perhaps as if he is about to cry or has just finished crying. Probably just about to cry—there is something like disbelief in his face. It is 2002 and his foot is worth several million pounds. Something knocks at you from the wrong side, from the inside. You close your eyes, and Beckham's gleaming shin guards stay with you, ghost your retinas for a moment, then dissolve.

World Trade Center/Head

You meet a friend for dinner at Molly's, which is full of the usual regulars—undocumented Irish construction workers and investment bank lackeys: the administrative assistants and data enterers and mailroomies. You are eating a medium-rare burger with one hand and decadently smoking with the other. It is almost as if you intuit that this won't be possible for very much longer. You haven't been following it, but the bill will be passed in December, the bars and restaurants, smoke-free by spring.

You are on your second Guinness, which makes you want to put on music. You like Molly's juke because it has the most Pogues albums in the city, plus it's been one of those days—frequent lately, it seems. You feel funny but you don't know why. You don't even know what you mean by funny. Which is what you say when your friend, who is having the shepherd's pie and also smoking, asks. Tomorrow's the anniversary, he reminds you. How have you worked in an office all day, printing letters and time-stamping materials to be copyedited and proofed, penciling dates in your boss's calendar even, without seeing?

I walked, he says without prompting, seven miles home to Brooklyn. I drank an entire bottle of whiskey that night. When I woke up the next morning I thought it had all been a nightmare. Really? you ask. No, he says, not really. I spent the night throwing up in my bathroom, completely sober.

So you didn't drink an entire bottle of whiskey?

No, I did that. But I didn't forget. That part's wishful thinking.

You weren't living here then so it's not your memory to share, but you listen to him talk a little more about the dust and the fear and the posters, some of which still hang in gray swelled strips on the lampposts and scaffolds around town. They are unreadable now, but no one will take them down. As you listen, something uneasy swells inside you. The room darkens a bit and the sound of the other patrons is suddenly deafening. You stand up, unsure of where you are going, until he puts a dollar in your hand and requests "Fairytale of New York."

The jukebox swims in front of you—you can't make out

the numbers next to the track listings and you seem to be having trouble drawing a full breath. The door is two feet away and you leave the jukebox queued with money to get some fresh air, to get out of this cave for just a minute.

The street is empty, and in the deepening dark of the night, you see that the blue lights are on. There is no cloud cover tonight, so they rise up from Ground Zero as far into the sky as you can see. You wonder if there are astronauts out there right now and if they can see these other twin towers, these ghosts. You have never looked at them for very long because, even though you have no religion, and the thought is frankly stupid, you are afraid that if you look at the lights long enough, you will see the spirits of the dead being sucked up in them, like some tractor beam to heaven, a pneumatic salvation. Like jumping off a building in reverse. You try to take a deep breath but your breath won't come. The lights go out.

When you come to, you see the upside-down faces of strangers and, between two of their heads, the blue lights. You are extremely confused. If someone asked you your name, you would not be able to say. There is no sound but a soft ringing. Then your friend's head juts into view and his voice cuts through the white noise: What happened? Where'd you go? Jesus Christ, you're bleeding.

You decide not to say anything until someone tells you what's going on. Your friend sets you up and cradles you and puts a napkin—where did he get the napkin?—to your chin, and if you are glad for something, it's that the tower lights have left your field of vision. You sit on the sidewalk while concerned people bird-walk around you and make noise on their phones and then there is an ambulance and then you are inside it and your friend holds your hand and your hair when you throw up into a white bag, but until you turn to go crosstown to Bellevue, to stitches and the diagnosis of a concussion, and some half-baked hypotheses about undercooked meat and low blood sugar, you make yourself look at those two lights through the portholes in the back of the ambulance doors, as if your looking could mean anything at all.

Empire State Building/Phallus

You have been inside twice now and up to the top once, but you can't remember much of the trip except that the lobby ceilings seemed too low, too gray, and the elevator went so fast your ears popped. When you think of the Empire State Building, it is always an exterior view, jutting beyond the tops of the Village brownstones, a guiding beacon at night, when the streets creep together and the city rearranges itself. When the grid seems to disappear, there is always that great glowing pyramid tip. They change the lights on it according to the seasons or holidays, but in your mind, it always glows red, white, and blue—a sign of American optimism, a great anchor of capitalism, that directional daddy, standing guard.

You look at it now, reassured you're headed north. This part of the city feels friendly. The old tenements crouch close. The shop windows are lit and full of the kinds of business you never have need for—a stationery shop, a designer pet clothing boutique, a restaurant that serves thirty-dollar macaroni and cheese. It is not even late, only freshly dark, which is why you are not scared, but merely surprised, when the passenger door of a semi cab parked on the street opens as you come parallel to it, and a man in a gray hoodie, eyes wide but expressionless, yells to you from the depths of the truck. He looks you straight in the eye and asks a simple question.

How does it look? he says. And you, stopped now, the Empire State eclipsed by the massive brow of the cab, can only ask, What? Your voice hangs in the air for a frozen moment and, in that moment, you see that the man has his cock in his hand, is yanking on it violently. You can't help but be transfixed by the head of it, squeezing past his white-knuckled hand. You realize that he is about to pull his own dick off in front of you.

Then the man is talking again, and automatically your eyes move back to his face. His own eyes are still wide, but now they are worried too. I'm going to see my girl, he says. But I been driving on mini-thins all night. Is it hard enough?

Your legs have realized, before your brain, that it is best to leave quickly, that the ladies selling French paper twenty feet away will not be able to help you should this man decide to drag you into his cab and make material his question. But really, no, that is not what you think. That is what you should have thought. On some level, your brain has responded mechanically to the danger, but consciously, the only situation you know that resembles this one is a joke. And so you laugh. You turn around and trip away nearly screaming with it. Later, you spend your last five dollars on a cab ride home.

Ridge and Rivington/Mouth

Your first mistake is that you are wearing headphones. You try to remember to take them off on the subway platforms and at night on the street, but there are so many rules to remember. This one sometimes escapes you, especially when you are listening to very good music, which occasionally makes you feel as if you are starring in a movie and the movie is your life, which is one of the more pleasant feelings New York inspires in you. Occasionally, New York makes your life feel much bigger and more interesting and possible than it is. This makes it easy to forget.

You are also wearing heels—the tall and tottering kind. You can't run in them—you can barely even walk. But you are walking, alone, from a bar in SoHo to your boyfriend's apartment on the Lower East Side because it is faster to walk across this part of town, even in tippy shoes, than to take a cab.

You see him first as you turn onto Delancey. He is walking alone. He wears a white T-shirt and a green stocking cap and looks like everyone else on the sidewalk tonight, which is why you forget him almost as soon as you see him. He drops back and you stutter-step onto your mix. It is only when you turn again onto Clinton that you sense someone behind you and stop to pretend to look at a menu in a restaurant window. You turn off the music, but leave in the headphones. Out of the corner of your eye, you see the man, the white T-shirt. He has turned the corner too, and he is walking slowly. You don't know if he slowed his walk when you stopped to read the menu, or if he has been walking that way this whole time and you are just being paranoid. But your paranoia is not unfounded—lately, more than usual, dead girls have been in the news.

In fact, you realize, as you read the description of a rosemary-lemon lamb risotto for the third time, that the bar you just left is very near The Falls, where, a couple weeks ago, that grad student was abducted and later found raped and strangled, bound with packing tape and dropped off near the Belt Parkway like a gift. And the actress, last year, not two blocks from your boyfriend's apartment, one block from where you stand right now. You were out that night too, doing what, you can't recall. You remember her last words from the newspaper though. What are you going to do, shoot me? she asked them. They did. This is how you remember to be good.

You should go into the restaurant. You should go into the restaurant and order a drink and call your boyfriend and tell him to meet you here. But when you look around again, the man is gone. You begin to get mad. This fucking city, you think. You tell yourself a joke. A girl walks into a bar...there is a punch line. Something to do with putting out, with being put out. The punch line is she didn't keep her mouth shut, of mouths taped shut, a bullet in the lung. You'll be goddamned if you'll slink into that restaurant. You turn and begin to walk determinedly up the street. You find your keys in your pocket and poke them like claws through your clenched fist. You clench your jaw to match your fist. Soon there are footsteps behind you again. You barely turn your head and get a glimpse of white cotton. The city thickens its breath.

Here's something funny you know: The Falls is owned by the Dorrian family. They also own Dorrian's Red Hand, which is where Robert Chambers met Jennifer Levin the night he walked her to Central Park, raped and bit her, then strangled her to death. Once, a man you were seeing took you to Dorrian's and you walked back to his place through the park, past where she was killed. He wanted to spook you. Just a bit of fun.

You are running unsteadily now, really more of a lope than a run—certainly this lead-assed shamble will not save your life. You can't hear him behind you over your own breath and the shod clop of your heels. Somehow, you manage to dial your boyfriend with your free hand. Open the door right now, you say as you round Rivington, his door half a block away. There is something in your voice because he doesn't say a word over the phone, but in a few more seconds you see him emerge onto the lit stoop. He is waving, but not smiling. You rush up the steps and pull him into the hallway and push the locked door shut behind you. There is no one on the sidewalk or the street, just your own reflection in the glass door, your pale, translucent face laid over the night, eyes like drill holes, lips parted and mute.

Manhattan/Hands

An Australian tourist has brought you here, has attached himself to you in the cold gray moments before dawn. You shiver in your down parka after so many hours in the club and that after-hours dive, and when he grips you closer, the feathers in your coat puff from the sudden pressure. You smell of sweat and whiskey and his cologne, something cheap and strong and chemical, but somehow not unpleasant. His hand twists softly in yours in a way that means he is about to say something.

Here's a spot, he says and stops walking and you both look around. Here? you ask. You are standing at Twenty-Third and Eighth, a monotonous Chelsea corner without charm or color. Your tongue is sore from the hours you've spent twisting it into improbable shapes in his mouth. You'd gone to Centro-Fly with some friends late last night, dressed to get the cover waived—something artfully shredded, glittering webs of fabric.

It happens every so often that you crave the kind of release you can find in a place like Centro-Fly, with all those beautiful strangers, each one a possibility. It doesn't even matter of what. What matters is by the end of the night you are abandoned to it all: the low lights and the bass pulse of the music, a sweaty flirtation in every corner, the anonymous press of curious limbs.

You don't know his name because he told you, but you couldn't hear, and so you asked him to repeat it and you still couldn't hear, but you nodded as if you had. This is probably why he calls you Love instead of your own name and you don't mind. He'd started a conversation by asking if you were French—the best pick-up line you'd ever heard, worthy of reward. You'd allowed him to buy you a drink and become quickly entangled in a misty corner of the club, all legs and mouths and fingers. Tomorrow, he will leave with his friends and return to Sydney and you will never see him again, and this is the way it should be—his presence now perfect because of the totality of his absence later.

He has brought you here to witness. There's this thing he'd read about in the paper yesterday, this thing that happens twice a year, once at dawn, once at sunset, where the sun aligns perfectly with the cross streets of the city, the grid, and…here he frowns.

And what? you ask, but he doesn't know. It's a thing you're supposed to see at least once in your life, he says, the sun barreling down the streets of Manhattan like a huge, spectral taxi.

Of course, you say. And there is nothing more important to you right now than to stand on this corner, next to this dark Baskin Robbins, and look down the tunnel of the cross street for the dawn. Sometimes, things are that simple. You smile as he puts his nose in your neck and sighs.

The streets are nearly empty this early on a Sunday morning, and this makes the city seem like a wilderness. As you watch, the sun begins its crawl over top of the edge of the East River. It angles through the tall, muddy buildings thrown up around it like canyons, as if they had always been there and always would be. The buildings on either side of the street seem to cup the sun, but cannot hold it, and they begin to disappear behind its needle-thin spikes, which creep toward you until they engulf you too, and you feel yourself begin to disappear. But when you look behind you, your shadows belong to giants. Your Australian smiles at you and, for a moment, you're in love, entranced, held by him, by the city, kept safe in these palms, and looking back down Twenty-Third Street, you think how the city proffers so many kinds of darkness, but here, on this corner, just now, a new kind of light.

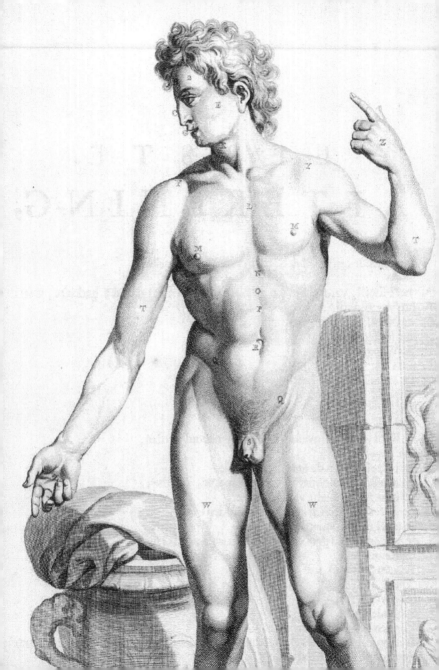

FELLOWSHIP

1. Seafood Night

Every Friday around five, we stack the sun chairs in the pump room of the Maple Hills Country Club and watch the servers from the restaurant roll giant table rounds down the paved walk between the tennis courts. They wobble across the pebbled pool deck and past the gazebo where we sit in black, regulation, one-piece suits. It takes three servers to handle a single round, to bang the rusted legs into place and hoist the table upright, to toss a white polyblend cloth over the entire surface with one snap. The buffets are brought down, the Sterno lit below them. And then: steaming steel trays filled with buttered corn cobs, the garlicky reek of Oysters Rockefeller, yawning mussels and pink whole lobsters, the faint bleached tang of cooked mollusk shell. Never mind that the nearest body of water is the catfished Iowa River. Every Friday, from five to nine, the club is a Cape Cod beach, and we—who have never seen the ocean, but find ourselves drawn toward water on some cellular level—perch on our lifeguard towers as if they are crow's nests, keeping our eyes on the water not for whales or land, but for children whose fearlessness makes them susceptible to sinking.

We dream nightly of escape. We would like nothing more than to see Iowa rolling out its infinity in the rearviews of our farm trucks, our Civics or Metros (all shamed to street parking blocks away, to make room for the Lincolns and Caddies of the club guests). We rip through each *National Geographic* our grandfathers' yearly subscriptions provide. We pay attention to television and the news. Beautiful, violent things are happening a thousand miles east. And if the water inside us draws us to the water outside, in search of equilibrium, this is also true of our dark selves, the mystery of our desires, which can find nothing external to match the pressures they produce in us—not here, in the friendly width of these streets, these fields, these grocery aisles. Not in the open, incurious faces of the lobster eaters below. When their splashing children are finally banished and the pool closed, we climb down from our posts. While the servers disassemble the tables, we take the cold lobsters from the buffets—there are always extra—and crack them with our bare hands, sucking meat from tiny, flexible legs that split like fingernails.

The pool opens at ten but I'm supposed to be there at eight to set up deck chairs and check the garbage cans and test the water and fix the mix if it's off. Today, I arrive at seven. I haven't really slept since last night, when Mom and Dad called a "family meeting." It was pretty goddamned obvious what they were going to tell us. It's why James has been wetting his bed lately, and why I stole the *Titanic* picture from the family photo album in the living room and hid it in my old copy of *A Wrinkle in Time*.

Ian shows up at nine, late as usual. He's a swimmer on the college team and always has his shirt off, even when, like today, it's too cold. His back is ridiculous, an inverted triangle—shoulders wide and turned slightly in on themselves, held tight by the trapezius, incredibly pronounced from all his hunching through the water. He's also stoned, as usual. He staggers down to the pool deck, dropping Visine into his eyes as he goes. I always get a little nervous when he's on the pool deck, on first position, on the stand by himself.

"Hey kid," he says with an easy smile as tears run down his face. I'm pretty sure he doesn't know my name.

"Ian," I say, "pH levels are good. I didn't get to the cans yet though, so…"

"No problemo, chica." He waves and wanders across the pool deck to the first garbage can. It's not that I haven't

21

checked the cans—in fact, before Ian showed up, I walked around kicking the trash cans, making sure to take all the pressure on the hard rubber toe of my tennies and yelling, "Fuck you!" every time, imagining my father's soft, bearded face. He seemed the unhappiest of all of us, and this made it easy to blame him.

In one of the cans, the one by the wading pool, something shifted inside when I kicked. I drew the hinged top back and found two stupid eyes peering up at me. The thing hissed and I flipped the lid back down.

I've kind of forgotten about it until I see Ian's shadow fall long into the concrete slab of the women's bathroom, where I'm stocking the toilet paper with shaking hands, wondering what's going to happen to my brother who isn't yet old enough to realize what huge assholes his parents have become.

"Critter alert," Ian says.

The philosophy of work at the pool is smelt it/dealt it. I let Ian think he's found the raccoon. I grab the skimmer off its hooks on the perimeter fence and follow him across the deck and through the little wooden gate to the baby pool area. He kicks the garbage can and there's a skittering—claws on the heavy plastic lining. He'll have to lay the can gently on its side and then get out of the way quickly, in case the coon is angry or rabid. I tell him I have his back and hold the skimmer defensively in front of me like a hockey goalie.

"Shit," he grunts, and squats the can to the ground.

"Get out of the way." I wave the net at the can.

"Jesus, get closer," he says. "I think it's coming out."

As if we're watching some sunny-day, rich-people horror movie, paws grasp the plastic lip and the raccoon emerges, spiky and damp and humping itself onto the length of the can, Ian sort of frozen, watching it. I try to shake my head free of the buzz I haven't noticed all morning until now, but my reaction time is messed up.

The raccoon seems to be checking out Ian, looking him up and down in a leisurely, half-interested way, and then it lunges toward him. Ian makes a kind of hoarse squawk and jumps backwards. Unstuck by his yell, I leap forward, brandishing the aluminum pole, and get the raccoon's head in the net, while it latches itself, all paws and teeth, onto the skimmer. I run to the baby pool and plunge the thing into two feet of water. The raccoon thrashes and I—or not me, but some reptilian part of me I've never met before—smash the skimmer to the bottom again and again, until feel a brittle, twiggy snap. The animal goes limp in the netting, its back probably broken. I feel like I might throw up.

Ian comes up beside me. He cranes his neck to look into the pool. He doesn't want to get too close to it or to me.

23

"Holy fuck," I pant.

"You killed it."

My chin is starting to do this involuntary crumple that means I'm about to cry. "I didn't mean to."

"You looked like you meant to."

I drop the skimmer and it's so loud on the pavement I have to bring my teeth together to settle the vibration in my head. The raccoon looks smaller underwater—no way it was an adult. I look at it, and think, *I killed that.* Ian offers to clean up and I go sit in the gazebo, at the pool entrance, where people sign in and pay their guest fees.

When he comes up later and asks if I want to go home, the question makes me cry harder. And when I shake my head and wipe my nose on the sleeve of my lifeguard sweatshirt, he says, "Come to the pump room," and I do because he looks confused and afraid, like I too might rise up and claw him, and I realize he thinks I'm crazy, all fucked up over a baby raccoon, and so, when we squat on two bulbous gray metal meters, growing out of the pump room floor, I tell him about last night, about my parents. I use the word they kept using—*separation*—a word that is pointedly not *divorce.* I would rather it not be Ian who knows this before anyone else, but there is no one else. He doesn't say anything. In the dank, chlorine reek of the room, his lighter glows under the

24

ANATOMIES

joint he's brought for us, and the pain in my chest as I suck in smoke feels like something to be thankful for.

Two hours later, I'm still red-eyed and dry-mouthed, but tear-free, sitting in the club gazebo in a manner I hope conveys both alertness and innocence. To the club mothers of Maple Hills, I want to look like the opposite of a person who would smoke weed on her guard shift. The reflective lenses in my sunglasses help—in my face the mothers see only themselves—but I realize I'm conveying too much alertness when Wendy Comstock glances up while she's signing in and then edges the clipboard nearer to herself as if to protect the privacy of her signature and club number. As if there'd be anything to do with her club number if I did steal it. Maybe a lesson with the golden tennis pro, a tan Swede straight off the cover of a romance novel. I'm imagining him bending me over the net and spanking me lightly with a racket, when a tall boy with large, rubbery features and long eyelashes wanders up to the gazebo and signs in himself and his little brother, who looks like he's about the same age as my brother, James. The older one smiles and that's all it takes. The heat, the weed, the thoughts of the tennis racket, and probably, perversely, even the news of the separation have all undone me. I feel hazy and discombobulated and like the only thing

25

that will make it all better is to be pressed against this guy as soon as possible. Phallically, I need a single point of focus. When the boys and their hairless and tawny bare chests have swept past the gazebo, I pull the sign-in sheet toward me and spin open the Rolodex to find their family info: Wychensky, Wayne and Donna. Ted & Liam.

I must have given off some pheromone, because when the third guard shows up at noon and Ian relieves me at the gazebo for my snack bar rotation, the older brother—Ted or Liam?— buys a pack of M&Ms, but manages to look, somehow, like he couldn't give a shit about actually eating them.

"You have to eat them fast, or they'll melt all over you." I try to say this in a suggestive way.

"Actually, M&Ms were invented not to melt. For soldiers in World War II. The candy shell?"

Simultaneously, I feel like, *You've got to be kidding me*, and, *I totally want to fuck you*. And somehow he gets it, because he blushes, then grins and sticks the bag of candy in the pocket of his damp trunks and walks away. Hours later, I'm on first position and the little brother comes up to the stand with his hand cupped over his eyes like a sailor. I make him stand there because my whistle and my sunglasses and my great height on the lifeguard stand tends to scare kids and I'm not above enjoying that.

26

Finally, I acknowledge him with a nod.

"I'm Liam," he says.

"Hi Liam. I'm Sarah."

He's brown as an almond and his hair is curly and dark. He looks like Disney's Aladdin and I'm sure someday he'll be as hot as his brother. Hotter, probably.

"My brother says he thinks you're pretty."

I make no expression and don't even move my head, but I find Ted with my eyes. He's rubbing sunscreen on his stomach like it's the most interesting and difficult thing he's ever done.

Ted picks me up from work that night in his Chrysler LeBaron, and some time later, but perhaps not enough time, his chewed-at fingertips are fumbling their way past my underwear, and the smell of chlorine is all around us, and all of a sudden, I have a new summer project that doesn't involve sitting around feeling sorry for myself.

In the next few weeks, we establish a routine: on my nights off, we go to a movie, maybe for pizza, and then we motor out somewhere more or less deserted and take off our clothes. Soon, Ted has nuzzled, licked, and put his fingers on and in almost every fevered part of me, but he refuses intercourse.

One night, I bring out a joint after we pull into a fallow field off the gravel road that winds behind a half-finished housing development. The cicadas chatter around us and hundreds of lightning bugs hang chest high, at the top of the seeded grass, flashing their semaphore. I bop Ted gently on his beautiful Roman nose with a red Bic and twiddle the joint at him from my other hand. He takes the lighter and throws it out the window. "I'm not down with chicks who use."

"What?" I pull back the joint before he can chuck it too.

"No drugs, babe. Them's the rules."

"Why are you talking like that? Whose rules?"

He looks less sure of himself, his huge Adam's apple bobbing. "Pastor John's."

"Oh fuck, *that* guy?"

Pastor John is a balding twenty-something who plays Pearl Jam covers on his acoustic guitar and speaks motivationally at our high school once a year. He runs a popular crosstown evangelical ministry for the kinds of kids who have great skin and expensive cars and a brand of stupid, beautiful arrogance that almost takes your breath away. They get high on life and go to Very Good State Schools. Ted's one of them—he'll be off to Madison in the fall, which is close enough to pain me with a glimmer of hope that our summer thing might outlast the summer.

28

"Are you in his…teen group or whatever?"

"Youth group, and yes, I go to his Friends and Fellowship Fridays."

Ted sounds defensive and he should be. This is Pastor John we're talking about. During last year's all-school assembly about self-respect, he performed a country version of "Ice, Ice Baby," in which he changed the lyrics of the chorus to *Nice, nice baby*. He frequently organized awkward and probably dangerous trust falls, and preached abstinence whenever he got the chance. Pastor John's biggest message is that intercourse is disrespectful of a girl's body and the holy sanctity of marriage. Thank weeping baby Jesus, Ted follows only the letter of this law.

I try, I try, I do. I beg and plead and prance and suck and tease, but Ted is adamant. We seem to reach some sort of stalemate about sex, but I manage to disappear into him anyway. His LeBaron, my salvation. Most nights of the week, I slide into my mother's dark house late and pretend not to hear her weeping through her bedroom door. I imagine a future for myself full of adult things but without adults.

2. Trial Separation

In the early days of divorce, when it's still being referred to as a trial separation, it seems that everyone does everything wrong. After swearing we won't, we bring up custody. Some of us wake at night in cold wet beds and cry out, and others of us ignore those cries which seem to come from a planet we don't want to inhabit, which sound to our cringing ears like a symptom of some infectious disease we don't want to come down with. Decisions are made and boxes are packed. Some of us are upset that others of us are taking all the records and hi-fi equipment, but these complaints are deftly turned inside out and become reasons to visit the new place, the new living situation, the new beige-and-black-leather townhouse monstrosity with Berber wall-to-wall and white plastic vertical blinds that hang like blades and dissect the view of the spewing water feature in the center of the pond behind the development.

We seem to be unbecoming a *we*. We seem to be becoming an *us* and a *them*, but even on either side of this dividing line, we each stand alone, tucked into ourselves, the distance between us—even those of us on the same side, those of us who did not royally fuck up and irrevocably ruin it for the rest of us—enormous and growing with each passing, teary day. We hear each other's clotted breath in the night. We no longer eat dinner together. We sit in the basement, pushing our injection-molded He-Men against each other (in love or hate, we don't know), and wait for the rest of us to join in, but we are scattered and wounded, and in our pain, turn away from each other. Others of us see the slinking about and the downward cast of the eyes, and we understand at once. We try to sound patient and convincing: *No one has ever died from this. Lots of people go through this. We'll all be okay.* What we really want is to run away. What we really want is for those of us who are children to stop acting like children, even though this is impossible and—ironically, hypocritically—a childish wish.

For the first time in years, we are truly alone. We clip our nails and toenails carefully—there seems to be all the time in the world now for personal grooming. We feel happy for a few days to finally be free of the dog hair, but after a few more days, we realize how awfully we miss the dog. It's the dog that finally sends us to our knees, and our hands to our head in front of the vertical blinds in the middle of one long, dogless night. When we look up again, we realize we are staring at the light on the water feature and that the color of the light is changing as we stare. We watch it go from green to blue to purple to pink to red to orange to yellow to green to purple

31

until our lashes dry and our fists unclench.

The summer's a long slow yawn. James and I are at Dad's two-bedroom apartment every weekend, which is actually more family time than any of us have ever spent together. It feels like prison.

Dad doesn't have a couch, just a low glass coffee table in front of the TV, an ancient half-ton wood monstrosity with side panels and knobs, which sits on the floor, like us. James and I eat Cheetos off the coffee table from a family-sized bag. We've already watched our old pirated copies of *Beauty and the Beast* and *Clue*. Halfway through *Tucker: A Man and His Dream*, the TV screen fuzzes over and when the picture returns, there's a topless woman with sky-high blonde bangs kneeling between the legs of a hairy man with his pants around his ankles. The man places one big mitt on her head, crushing the anemone-like structure of her hair. Dad flies up, blocking the screen, and fiddles at the control panel of the TV. A wet smacking sound precedes the silence.

"What was that lady doing?" James asks.

I can feel Dad looking at me for help. He's always been short with us, impatient. His temper was a force that filled our house with its sound and fury, and it seems to me he's been the chief composer of our misery. I do not want to help him, but I feel protective of my little brother, so I ask James if he wants to watch *Clue* again, which is his favorite movie, and he says yes yes like the six-year-old he is, and when I settle back next to him, Dad gets off the floor and retreats to the kitchen. I don't know exactly what he's doing back there. Pots rumble and the kitchen faucet runs. I hear the fridge smack open, twice. It's not enough, though—even from the other room, Dad's shame fills the apartment like gas from a leaky stove. I look at the TV screen and narrow my focus to the wavering, over-red images. It's a kind of meditation, except instead of calm and peace, I allow myself to fill with a rage so heavy it pins me to the ground.

It's a long time before I can stand again, and when I do, I find the rage has not abated. I grab my keys and stomp to the door. I tell them not to wait up and snarl that I'll sleep in my own bed, in my own fucking house. James is a perfect replica of my father: the O's of their mouths, their eyes like wounds. I open the door and no one stops me, so I slam it hard and feel, for one second, like I've won.

An hour later, Ted and I are parked at the spillway. Ted is doing this thing in my vagina where he rubs one finger up and down the other, producing what I imagine is supposed to be some sort of crickety vibrato. I don't know where he gets his fancy ideas, but I don't want to hurt his feelings either.

33

I arch my head back toward the half-open window to get a sniff of the barbeque smoke coming from a nearby campsite. All day, I've only eaten Cheetos. Ted takes my contortions as encouragement and the cricket quickens.

"Hey," I say after a few more minutes of this. "Let's go outside and look at the tube." The tube is a mad explosion of water that rushes over the dam gate at 3500 cubic feet per second according to my physics teacher, Mr. Bellows, and though our car is parked slightly upstream, it's a fairly easy walk, even in the dark, up the hill to the banked bridge directly over the outflow. Standing there, you feel as though you might be sucked into its deafening, fishy roil.

Recently, before the announcement, but when things were already bad, when Mom and Dad stomped around their bedroom every night and bellowed at each other like a couple of cows about to be slaughtered, I was picking through a family photo album, trying to remember a time when their anger hadn't rumbled every wall in the house, and I found a snapshot of them standing above the tube in the golden light of an early autumn afternoon, the day we all went fishing together—maybe three or four years ago. I remember James was fascinated by the way Dad hooked the worm. Later, he spent the car trip home saying teary prayers for each dead worm and the grieving worm families they'd left behind.

34

ANATOMIES

In the snapshot, my mother's leaning against the chest-high chain link that surrounds the dam gate. Her arms are spread at the shoulders like wings, and her hair, longer then and maybe darker, ripples behind her. My dad's hands are at her hips. They're doing *Titanic* at the top of the tube. I didn't realize how bad things had gotten until I saw that photo. And now, I can't even be here, can't pretend to enjoy my boyfriend's mediocre finger bang, without thinking about my parents and wondering what's to become of us all. I sigh and push Ted's hand away.

"Did you hear me?" I say. "Let's go up and watch the water."

"It's dark out—we could trip and hurt ourselves. Anyway, it smells."

In an instant, the rage is back and I am ready to push this thing to the brink. I know what it takes to hurt us both. "Why can't we just have sex like normal people?" I say. "I feel like a fucking freak out here."

Ted frowns. "You know I can't."

"Oh, right. Your pledge of chastity."

"It's important to me. You said you'd support me." He turns away, his modest erection wilting in his jeans, and starts the car. I pull up my shorts and thrust my pelvis as high in the air as I can to button them.

"I was just trying to get you to fuck me."

"Pastor John said you sounded like someone who'd resort to pressure tactics. And that I should be careful."

"You talked to him about me?"

"I didn't want it to be true, but now I see he was right—"

"What did you *say* about me?"

"—and I think…I don't think we should see each other anymore."

For the millionth time, I imagine Ted's legs spread out before me as I ride him like a combine; Ted's farmboy bulk squashing me into the crumb-sharp fabric of his back seat in an ironic missionary; Ted's ass tightening as he rams into me again and again. But now I see something else too: that asshole Pastor John staring at us with heaven's disapproval souring his face.

I elbow the door open and start walking toward the top of the tube, which looks like someplace furtive and ugly in Ted's headlights. Gravel, broken glass. I climb the steep spillway embankment and don't look back. He yells for me twice, then backs his car out and drives away.

Up here, at the top of the hundred-foot drop down to the churning, angry water, is the last place I saw my mother smile at my father. The Iowa River races furiously toward me. Beyond the dam, the reservoir is placid and has the rotten fertilizer smell of something dead.

36

3. Youth Group

In place of darkness, there was the fluorescence of junior high hallways. In place of demons, Zach Hellerman's man-sized fist sank into our stomachs. His spit hung, chrysalis-like, from the fringe of our bangs. Our glasses: bow-broken and skittered beneath a locker; our non-existent breasts: shamed; our prematurely large breasts: shamed; our balls: kicked back into the cavity of our bodies before they'd had the chance to fully descend.

After the darkness of our daily existence, the bread of our pain, who among us does not feel a huge unclenching inside, a sobbing relief, as we stare into the linoleum of the church basement floor and hear the stories rushing wild and full from each other like the river across the dam? We feel bathed in light. The peace we've been promised, for years, by parents and various administrators, most likely erstwhile bullies themselves, finally arrives in this unlikely and alien place which smells like the hospitalish rooms in which our grandmothers moan out the ends of their lives. How unlikely seems the bringer of our peace. His mousey goatee, the shaved head that we would later understand as an answer to balding, the way his voice twangs over the top of his acoustic guitar: too precise, show-choir trained, a fussy put-on. How

37

fitting that our savior here on earth, the man who would tell us about our savior up in heaven, would have the sort of head we would want to see punched, the kind of cringing attitude that would make us understand, finally, what was so hateful about ourselves.

And so, we have to learn to speak forcefully, to repulse the twin evils of drugs and sex—although many of us are still waiting, just waiting, for someone, anyone, to offer either. We've traded skin-care secrets and exfoliated ourselves to a rosy, Christian glow. We've kissed each other during church lock-ins, and at Camp Galilee, where we also learned that Mötley Crüe and Bon Jovi worship Satan, a lesson which Pastor John later encourages us to laugh off, but which nevertheless continues to freak us out. We have begun, some of us, to understand the price that such fellowship is asking—nothing less than our souls at the expense of our bodies. We have begun to fail each other.

One of us, just last weekend, tasted, finally, the seawater tang of his girlfriend's vagina—the Southern Comfort still hot in his belly—and ejaculated into his wrinkle-resistant Dockers. Another welcomed the sweet curl of methamphetamine into her lungs. We have turned eighteen and visited the Pleasure Palace with our non-youth-group friends and masturbated furtively into socks. There is, suddenly, a new vocabulary:

38

bong, dank, nug, DP, creampie, money shot, crystal, crank, tweak. Something inside us hungrily expands until we feel larger than our homes and schools and even, or especially, the basement of this church. We wake at night and touch our arms and legs and heads, certain they must have flown from us in sleep. We long to ask each other: Are we being devoured by lions or are we becoming them?

The corn is thigh high and I'm on my way to a church basement on the other side of town to eat crustless sandwiches and fraternize with the enemy. It's embarrassing, this sudden obsession. I've always prided myself on being cool with guys, less interested in a relationship than they were. The best thing about hooking up was the total-freedom feeling it gave me. Sex was something parents and school couldn't access or control. But Ted has beaten me; he's kept more of himself in reserve, has more secret rooms to which he's denied me access. He wouldn't let me in, but he let in Pastor John. I wanted to talk it out, but my calls went unanswered. I imagined he could hear my anger and desperation ringing out from under the bed, where he kept his phone, and that it repulsed him. He'd stopped showing up at the pool, though his brother still came. I was thinking about sending a note home with Liam, carrier-pigeon style, when I realized I could confront Ted, and possibly (in my fantasy) also Pastor John at a Friends and Fellowship Friday meeting. I would expose John as a weirdo and convince Ted to take me back. Dénouement make-up sex would follow in the pond at my dad's condo development. I got a sub for my Seafood Night shift and set out to win back Ted.

But Ted has stopped coming to youth group. At least that's what Pastor John tells me when I walk into the basement and interrupt a jam session between him and three groupies. The bongos guy I recognize from school, but the other two kids are strangers, though the girl on guitar smiles at me. The friendliness of the group flusters me. Instead of introducing myself and calling out Pastor John for being a fraud, I say, "Um…where's Ted?" and they look confused.

John rises, his pukka-shell necklace slapping against the collar of his t-shirt, and says, "Haven't seen him in a few weeks. What's your name?"

I tell him and think I see a squint of recognition.

He says, "God's casa es su casa, Sarah. Have some snacks. We usually jam until most of the group gets here. Then I call everyone to fellowship."

I nod and walk toward the spread of drinks and food on the other side of the room, trying to avoid talking to anyone while the sunny creeps behind me sing, "I don't need no doctor, all I need is Jesus's love." I drink cranberry juice from a Dixie cup and separate a long stick of mozzarella from itself, string by awkward string, as more eager kids file in and take up the joyful noise. When the music stops, I have just dragged a large piece of caulifower through the dip in the center of the vegetable tray and put the whole thing in my mouth. In this new silence, it feels as if the protective covering around me has been torn away. A tambourine jangles faintly as its master puts it down. Pastor John yells into the calm and heavy air, "My lord, lift me up to be with you! My lord, call me and I will answer!"

I try to slow my stuttering heart as I turn from the buffet toward the youth group. They're all sitting there with eyes closed, smiling. John's hands are extended to the ceiling and they jitter, as if he's been struck with a neurological disorder.

"Tonight, we thank you for bringing us a new lamb, named for the wife of Abraham! Sarah! Sarah, come here, Sarah, and say the Lord's name with us!"

They open their eyes and look at me like puppies, and I realize they've left a notch of their prayer circle open for me on the mat. I point to my bulging cheek and keep chewing as though answering a question no one has asked. They keep looking and I keep standing there, pointing at my face, finger like the barrel of a gun, chewing, chewing, unable now to

41

swallow as they stare, the creamy dip curdling against my tongue. My head is filled with the noise of my mouth but I can tell the silence that binds us together is very awkward indeed.

"Sarah!" yells John, and a piece of cauliflower lodges itself in my windpipe. There's a long moment, as I try to draw my breath to cough, when nothing happens. My body feels as though it has always been here and always will be and I'll spend the rest of my life in this basement being stared at by Christian youth, me staring back—curiosities to each other, zoo animals watching zoo animals. The guitar girl's mouth moves, and from a distance and several seconds delayed, I hear the words, "She's choking?" and then I'm on my knees, the cauliflower paste coming out of my mouth as I open it to the ground, and then someone strong and hippie-fragrant is kneeling behind me, enfolding me in a great hug, and the cauliflower is cutting a path back up my throat, and there's the sound of my own wheezing life and pain in my knees and my lonely sinner's blood pulsing hot in my ears. Like a newborn, I breathe and then I cry. The group makes noises around me and someone asks if they should call an ambulance, and then I uncurl myself from the cement floor, clear my throat, and walk out of the worship room like Lazarus from his cave.

I think about driving to Ted's house, but I know what

42

I'd find: a big happy family playing Yahtzee, the Rolexed arm of Ted's father slung around his tastefully small mother, their slippers, in the loafer style, parked side by side. Liam would say something child-wise and they'd laugh together like the stars of their own sitcom, like they were on their own cloud up in heaven and had forgotten the rest of us, down here, in our weird, hungry bodies on earth.

Instead, I take the country road out of town for a while, just to remind myself that I can. I drive until the road Ts into a highway. I wonder how much driving it would take to hit big water, how much of a relief that might be.

James is already in bed and Dad's bent awkwardly over the dishwasher when I let myself into the apartment. I take a beer from the fridge and sip it at the kitchen bar. It burns my throat. Dad doesn't say anything about the beer, so I tell him about Ted and how we broke up and I say I even went to his youth group, but it's like he's just disappeared from my life. And is this always going to happen, this disappearing? And what about you? Are you going to disappear too?

Really, I don't ask that, even though I want to manufacture a father-daughter moment. I want things to all feel okay again, just for a minute. But I also know this would be a lie.

43

"Better luck next time," Dad says as he closes the dishwasher door. "I'm going to bed."

Does anything sound cozier than a dishwasher at night? Even in this sad bachelor wreck of a place, where each of us is tucked into our own separate corners like water molecules—bonded for a moment, but always breaking apart.

I open another beer. The VHS tape marked *Tucker* is still sitting on top of the TV. I let the slow motor of the VCR suck the tape into its broad, flat mouth. I turn the volume all the way down. I sit on the floor and listen to the rhythmic slosh and hiss of the dishwasher. I watch through to the end.

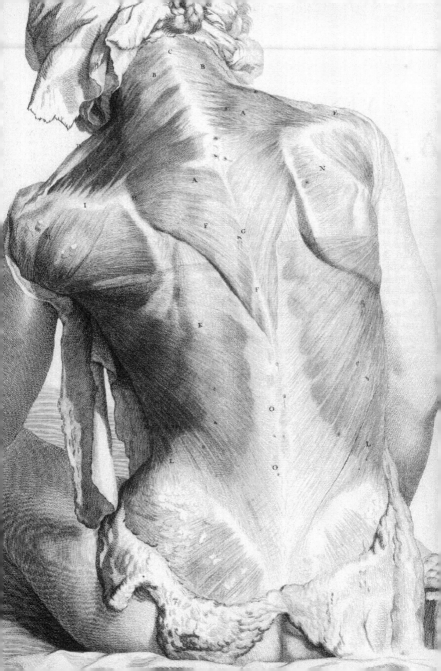

INDIRECT OBJECT

The ACT tutor selects another binder from the shelf. On the spine of the binder is his student's name: Mackenzie H. Currently, there are three Mackenzies attending the tutoring center, the others being Mackenzies S. and G. What can account for the popularity of the name? He can only think of Spuds Mackenzie, the beer dog from the eighties. Surely this is not the Mackenzie fountainhead. It's an ugly name— unlyrical, masculine, ahistorical. Later, if he remembers, he will Google it.

In the front of Mackenzie H.'s binder is the subject and the book chapter he's assigned to teach her today: Reading 2. This is their fifth meeting. He's also teaching her English and Science, although "teach" is maybe not the right word. He reads to his students from the book that the for-profit testing center he works for has developed, though "reads" is not the right word either because the tutor goes to pains to disguise the fact that he's reading the book aloud. What he does is he speaks aloud the things the center wants his students to know about taking the ACT. He does this while looking at the side of his students' slack and zitty faces. The things he says are his own words but the ideas are borrowed. The sessions vacillate between speaking (the tutor) and taking timed practice tests (the students).

Sometimes, the tutor asks a student a question:

"What's the main idea of this passage?"

"Like, there's…um, there's the independent…the Declaration of Independence and it…"

The last word stalls. This is one kind of silence. The tutor is intimately acquainted with it by now.

"What about it?"

"Um, it's the Declaration of Independence so it's about independence and how it's declared for our freedom."

"Well…okay, the passage is about the Declaration of Independence, but in what way?"

"Like, for our freedom in the revolutionary war?"

"No, that's not— Look, in your own words, what's the passage about?"

A silence so total the tutor looks up from the book to make sure the student is still there.

"The Declaration of Independence."

"And?"

"And…our freedom to have independence to be declared?"

"The passage is about how the Declaration of Independence was moved to a bunch of different locations and now it's where?"

"It's. Um."

"That last paragraph?" He taps on the paper—*tap tap tap*—to crowd out the silence.

"Oh. Um. It's. At the Nat—the National Archive."

Chive. Like the herb.

It's not that the students are stupid. Well, maybe some of them are, but he can tell that a lot of them are quick from the way they stumble through the swamp of the language, the way they blindly string together words from the text, the way every sentence ends in a question mark because of the panicked question implicit with each answer: "Does what I'm saying even make sense?" He can tell they just don't read, and because they don't read, language does not illuminate for them: it befuddles. So far, not a single student he's asked can remember the title of the last novel they read. He used to ask what they read for fun but got nowhere with that. Now he asks what they read for class, but it's as if he's asked them what they think of Wittgenstein's truth function for all the blank looks they give him. Sometimes he wants to ask that instead. If he did, if he asked them, they would try to

49

answer. They always try to answer. They don't want to think about anything—in fact, he sometimes doubts their ability to think at all, these children of the internet—but they all, always, attempt to answer. For Wittgenstein, the opacity of language was a problem to be solved. The tutor had been writing his dissertation on Wittgenstein. An impossible task, his committee had warned him, given the time and funding available. Wittgenstein would have hated these children— probably would have hit them as he was wont to do in his day—but he might have understood their fear.

And why should these kids know how to think if no one has ever taught them? That is not his job. His job is to help them score an average of five points higher on the ACT so that they will be eligible to go to college where their academic, if not intellectual, handicaps will become someone else's head-slapper.

Some version of this narrative unwinds itself in the tutor's head each day he works, which is every day except for Sunday when the center is closed because the franchise owner is an evangelical Christian, but today it feels as though the tutor's resentment is really given the room to bloom and grow in his soul. His first client (the franchise owner does not like this word, but it is more honest than "student," so the tutor thinks of them as clients, even if, at work, he refers to them, aloud, as students), Peter M., is a greasy, stooped boy, who makes a game of underenunciating his answers and then, when the tutor asks him to repeat himself, Peter rudely (it seems to the tutor) and loudly overenunciates, which gives the tutor the odd feeling of being embattled, but instead of arguing about anything, Peter is only, for instance, defining the scientific method, furiously and with the sibilance of a snake. By the end of their session, the tutor is fantasizing about smacking an expression onto Peter's sacklike head.

After Peter comes Mackenzie H., in a pair of gold-sequined Uggs. The tutor makes a little hatch mark on the first page of her file. According to his count, this is the ninth different pair of Uggs she has worn to her sessions. When it had become clear several weeks ago that his student was wearing a different pair of puffy, aesthetically displeasing boots to each session he had with her, and coordinating her outfit based on each pair, he performed a cursory internet search, and from what he understands, Uggs (how strangely appropriate the name: that comic-book sound of disgust, that premier syllable which begged for its suffix, -ly) were very expensive. Even the knockoffs were nearly a hundred dollars. The tutor did not suppose he had bought a thousand dollars worth of shoes in his entire adult life. Certainly not since becoming a graduate student, ten years ago. Since the problem with his funding last year, he was, in fact, struggling a bit to buy meat, now that gas was on the rise again. He lived a half hour from the testing center when traffic was light.

And this was probably just a sampling of her entire shoe wardrobe. Surely, she did not wear the things through the wilting Midwestern summers. Mackenzie slumped into the green plastic chair beside him. "Hi," he said and one side of her face went up as if he'd just given her news about which she was highly skeptical.

"I didn't do my homework. I was just too busy. It was like, I had cheer tries and this city college scholarship thing I had to write a whole paper for, so I just didn't get to read about the different kinds of passages or whatever." She manages to sound accusatory, as if the tutor is to blame for this. He makes another tick mark on the first page of her file. They are never to castigate the students themselves. He would tell the center director, instead, who would tell the parents who could then choose to punish or not, since they were paying for the whole setup in the first place. The tutor makes his face a mask and does not give her the satisfaction of his own penal impotence. *Penal impotence*, he thinks and coughs into his fist.

"Okay, the four kinds of reading passages are social sciences, humanities, natural sciences, and prose fiction." *Prose fiction*. He hated the clunky redundancy the term seemed to carry with it. It confused the students, although pretty much everything confused the students. *Confused students.* There was another redundancy. Stated as an analogy: fiction is made of prose just as students are made of confusion. Unfortunately, there are no analogies on the ACT.

He tells Mackenzie to do her homework now, in front of him. She reads four passages and he skims them with her so that he can ask her questions about them. The humanities passage is a brutal piece of business jargon, a parody of itself. It is, in fact, completely devoid of humanity.

He asks her the main idea of the prose fiction passage, which is the beginning of *Invisible Man* by Ralph Ellison. He asks her to tell him the correct order of events which scientists use to describe the eventual death of our star, the sun. He says, "I'm going to read you part of one passage and you tell me the main idea. *In today's markets, leveraging best practices in order to improve margins above and beyond those of the competition necessitates constant assessment and reassessment.*"

"What emptiness," he thinks. He thinks of his Ludwig. *What we can say at all can be said clearly.* If Wittgenstein was alive today, he would definitely kill himself, like three of his brothers before him.

Mackenzie answers each question without actually proving that she has retained a shred of information from or

53

impression of any of the passages. He gets the notion that she had just been sitting there, staring at the test booklet margins for fifteen minutes rather than reading the passages. When he asks her a question, her eyes skitter, panicked, across the page, and she spits out words as she sees them in the text, hopping from one important-sounding word to the next, stringing together sentences with incorrect prepositions, running across the bridge of her answer as it collapses under her. This is how it goes for an hour. As she skulks out of the room at the end of their session, her Uggs wink at him under the fluorescents, as if they are flirting with him, and he sees in a flash how she will grow up to be a selfish and incurious adult, probably while making a lot of money. How she would trade her Uggs for breathtakingly expensive heels and pay someone to wax her pubic hair. He sees the pink cocktails. Maybe she would aspire to appear on *The Bachelor*. She might make a good Bachelorette. He can see she will perform the signs of cultural femininity without being particularly attractive, yet she will read to other adults as attractive, even if her skin is orange, and her lips too pink. He makes his final marks on her chart and puts her binder aside. He picks up the next binder in his pile, makes a mark on the front page of his chart and waits for the next client to appear.

★

The tutor pokes his head out of the tutoring lab and scans the waiting room. It is Tuesday at four, Peter's usual time, but no Peter.

He sits at his tutoring table and draws lopsided prisms in his notebook. He draws a dog sitting, a side view. He draws a car that seems to be going somewhere but isn't. He draws a crude map of the world and fills in the continents so that they look like turds. He puts a dot in the middle of the North America turd. You are here. Here you are. Here. The sound of students saying stupid things is all around him, choking him. The air is out of the room, which smells strongly of pencil shavings and reheated meat gravy which wafts out into the tutoring room from the kitchenette. He puts Peter's binder back and tells the front desk he's a no-show. When he gets home, the tutor eats a frozen pizza and watches *The Apprentice* and feels superior to the vapid, conniving people on the show, to the dummies watching the show, to the people who are tricked into thinking they feel anything for the connivers, who are not people as much as caricatures of people. "People." Like that. In scare quotes. He watches TV and feels superior to practically the whole country, which is the only way he knows to make up for the loneliness.

★

Peter misses another session and the tutor is called into the office by the enigmatic, evangelical learning-center franchise owner.

"Listen, there's a problem with Peter."

"A problem?" Inexplicably, the tutor's pulse quickens.

"He won't be coming in any more."

"Okay..." The tutor wills him to say more, but the franchise owner stops there, with his mouth halfway open, as if wondering whether he should continue. The tutor prompts him: "Is it something I've done?"

The franchise owner closes his mouth and puts out his hands, "No no, nothing like that. Peter died."

"Oh."

"I wasn't going to tell you, but—"

"Why not?"

"What?"

"Why weren't you going to tell me?"

"I guess...I don't know. I'm not sure I thought it was appropriate conversation for the workplace."

"Okay."

"But here's the thing. Here's why I'm telling you now: The parents want to meet you."

"Me?"

"Yes—well. They're grieving and they want to, you know, they want to hear about their son. They want you to tell them about Peter."

"How'd he die?"

"Oh, I don't…that's not something we ask, here."

"When do they want to meet me?"

"Tomorrow. I've scheduled you for a four o'clock session with them."

"A session?"

"Yes, just pretend it's a regular tutoring block."

"Out there?" the tutor gestures at the open room full of laminated particleboard tables and mismatched plastic chairs with aluminum legs. On each table is an oversized clown-colored stopwatch. A tutor must use the stopwatch—never his phone or her own wristwatch—to proctor exams and practice tests for students.

The franchise owner shrugs, "Where else could I put you?"

"I don't know if I'm comfortable with this." But that is not exactly true. It would be more truthful to say the tutor does not feel anything about this or about Peter or his parents, including compassion, empathy, or any kind of largesse of sentiment. Technically, it is this feeling, this lack, that makes the tutor uncomfortable.

"But you knew Peter best."

The best of whom? The tutor cannot conjure Peter's face. Then he pictures himself slapping Peter, and there: there's the face.

"Okay."

Tonight, it's *Dancing with the Stars* and two half-hearted rounds of masturbation.

★

The parents are ashen, elsewhere to themselves, but entirely present to everyone else in the room. Their presence is alarming to the other tutors, who know why they're here, and to the students, to whom the appearance of parents—foreign, awkward, and uncomfortable, not to mention oversized for the scale of the room and the furniture in it—in the tutoring center was formerly unthinkable.

The tutor shows them to one of the open tables where he may or may not have worked with Peter on lab methodologies, or on the differences between subject and object.

"I love you," he had said once, antagonistically, to Peter, who had continued to stare at the table, but with a new, slightly different kind of veiled anger.

"What?"

"It's how to remember the difference. *I* is the subject because I am loving and *you* is the object because you are being loved. 'You' is the object of my affection."

"I is. I mean, I *am*."

The tutor's stomach shrank a little. "No, I didn't mean *you* you. I meant—"

He remembers the hard little sneer on Peter's face, and sees now how it was birthed from the larger, unconscious sneer of his father. The father is wearing some sort of heavy, furred coat—it may be cashmere or lambswool—and looking incredulously around the room like he detects a shit smell. The man puts a large hand on the fake wood-grain on top of the trapezoidal worktable. "This is where he...learned?"

Ha, the tutor wants to say. Ha ha ha ha ha.

"Sit." He pulls out the two small green plastic chairs for them and because the chairs are short, sized for children, Peter's parents lower somewhat unsteadily.

"Wait," booms the father, startling the mother who has only just regained her balance. "Where did Peter sit?"

The tutor puts his hand on the back of the wife's chair and accidentally touches the valley of her spine, which is knobbier than her general, maternal physique suggests.

"Here, he sat here, and I sat where you're sitting."

"Get up," says the father to the mother, who still has

59

not spoken and even now does not. There is hardly even a question in her eyes as she rises, steps to the whiteboard on the wall, and leans against it, clutching herself, like a person drowning in a dream.

The father swings his hips into the other chair and pats the open seat in front of the tutor. "Teach me," he says. And so the tutor sits down beside the grieving, sneering father, picks up a Reading curriculum binder, and begins to speak.

When they leave, the tutor notices that the dry erase marker from the whiteboard has transferred onto the mother's camel coat, the padded shoulder of which now reads backwards, *whom*. To whom, with whom, for whom. The tutor looks to the whiteboard but the preposition has been wiped away entirely.

★

The tutor does not know how to receive the father. That is to say, he doesn't mean to make the ambience in his apartment romantic, but there is no other readily available model for how to host, at least not available to the tutor. So when the father knocks on the door, a stick of incense and some candles are flickering in various corners of the room. The tutor's speakers shed John Coltrane's *A Love Supreme* into the air around them.

The tutor says, "Come in," and sweeps his arm over the dingy vista of his apartment. He says, "Have a seat," thinking the father will choose to sit at his small table in the kitchen because that's where the tutor usually sits, but instead he goes to the couch.

Besides the couch—a crumby brown chenille thing he'd picked up at Goodwill—there are only the two kitchen chairs. To get one and plop it down near the couch, while there's all that perfectly good couch real estate, all those cushions where the father *isn't* sitting, seems rude and alienating. But in equal parts, joining him on the couch seems overly familiar, too close. The tutor knows he can't hesitate too long, or his guest will begin to feel awkward, so he does the easiest thing and perches lightly on the other end of the couch. He sees that Peter's father has unfolded and is now carefully smoothing his cloth handkerchief onto his lap, as if he is a diner at a reasonably nice restaurant, instead of a stranger in a soupy-smelling one-bedroom apartment. The gesture makes the tutor extremely nervous.

"Thanks for penciling me in. I'm sure you're on a tight schedule." The father reddens, embarrassed by the obviousness of his platitude. The tutor and his apartment are clearly not on a very tight schedule, at least not one that involves, say, working to make money. "And I'm...I'm very glad you've been able to host this meeting. I want to do you a favor and cut right to the chase. My son." The man drops his eyes to his lap and swallows. "Were you and my son...involved?"

The tutor blinks and feels warm all over. Then he shivers. Then he is warm again. The man will not make eye contact with him. He just sits there in his fuzzy black overcoat with a hanky on his lap like a lunatic. The tutor feels set up. The father, on the voicemail from two days ago, had sounded lost, weak, in need of something that only the tutor could provide. Some strange measure of tutoring solace. Which was why the tutor had called him back—the tutor being moderately uncomfortable with the situation, but also in possession of a modicum of human empathy, and also somewhat bored.

When the father speaks again, his voice is low and he seems to be having trouble catching his breath. "I found his notebooks, his school notebooks and his ACT notebooks, from tutoring with you." The man reaches into a briefcase at his feet and pulls out three spiral-bound college-ruled pads, hands them to the tutor. The one on top is open to a page where Peter has penciled the equation for Newton's universal law of gravitation. The equation and its labels are orderly, but in the margins of the notebook, in twenty different styles and scribbled at all angles, is the tutor's full name. Over and over again. Here in cursive, there in block letters filled in with horizontal stripes, shiny with graphite. In the notebook below it, there are some grammar notes from one of their sessions. There is the phrase *I love you* with its subject and object labeled. Under that, Peter has written a series of sentences under the heading INDIRECT OBJECT:

- *I want to give him my love.*
- *I want him to love me.*
- *For him, I would do anything.*
- *Will he give me his heart?*

Then, further down the page, an impressively veined sketch of a spurting cock. The tutor feels heavy, as if, impossibly, the gravitational constant has increased.

"I didn't. I mean I would never." There is more stammering, which, the tutor realizes with frustration, makes him sound guilty. He takes a breath. "Listen, I had no idea your son had these feelings. I can't even—*nothing* like this even occurred to me, okay? This isn't me." Though clearly it was. "Maybe someone else?"

The father regards him silently for a long moment. "I believe you. When we found these, we hired an investigator. He's done a thorough background check on you. And Peter's

63

phone and email turned up clean. And the set-up at the center was so out in the open…"

"You've been investigating me?"

"He was my son."

The couch pings and the tutor looks up from the notebooks to see Peter's father has moved closer to him. The man shakes slightly; the tutor smells his sweat. The first side of the record has ended.

"I need to ask you… This is going to sound very odd, but—I didn't come here to threaten you. I wanted to. Well. My son, he felt love for you, or something like it. And he's gone now and it's somewhat my fault. Maybe," here, the man's voice cracks and he begins to cry, "maybe very much my fault."

The tutor puts a hand on his shoulder because what else can he do.

The man takes the hanky off his lap and presses it against his face, puts it down again, turns back toward the tutor and says, "Can I kiss you?" and then they are kissing, the father closing the distance without waiting for an answer, the hard fact of his teeth behind his lips, pressing painfully against the tutor's mouth, and then the invading tongue. The tutor puts his hand on the man's wet rough face but does not push it away. The kiss ends and the silence between them seems filled with possibilities, some exciting, some frightening, many a mix. It pulses like a heart or a star or something large in flight. And then the man is rustling through his apartment toward the door and his handkerchief has fallen to the floor like the trifle of a damsel and then he is gone.

★

Mackenzie H.'s Uggs are purple suede today. The tutor's seen them before, which seems to indicate that she has cycled through her entire collection, for now.

The tutor is feeling off-kilter. He sometimes gets a whiff of Peter's father, whose scent seems to be lingering in some crease, somewhere. A layer, silver and sharp, over a musk, the salt of a body. Stratosphere and troposphere. The tutor taps out the dactyls with the toe of his shoe.

He and Mackenzie are supposed to review some basic terms from biology. Mackenzie looks at the list and says, "I don't remember any of these."

"You don't really need to know them. You just have to read very carefully. The science test is really just another reading test. Read the passage in the workbook."

She reads the passage.

"Now tell me something about what alleles are and why

65

they're important."

She sighs. "I don't know."

"Anything."

"They're for genetics." She looks at him and he nods. "For the recessive ones? Or, like, the dominance?"

He puts his pencil down and takes a deep breath. All these children filling the air with their language. He thinks of Peter, of his inscrutability and his low, quiet voice. Peter already disappearing, disappeared.

Wittgenstein is suddenly in his mouth. "*What we cannot speak about, we must pass over in silence*," says the tutor.

"What does that mean?" asks Mackenzie.

"Think about it."

"I think it means—"

"No, don't answer. *Think* about it." Mackenzie doesn't say anything more, which he takes as participatory. "Close your eyes," he says and presses the button on his stopwatch.

"This is weird," she says and he shushes her again and she is quiet again and he sees her eyes really are closed and so he closes his too.

KINDNESS

"Hi Tom," says my girlfriend, Maggie, as soon as she opens the door, "How many people did you rape today?" Maggie has one of those noses that turns up at the end. In the summer, the bridge of it is covered in formless freckles that bleed into each other and across the tops of her cheeks. I try to kiss these places now, in rapid succession—cheek, nose, cheek—but she pulls away, pissed off. "How many?" She looks into my eyes and is completely still. In that stillness, I can see her getting ready. She is putting up her dukes. I sigh and walk into her kitchen and pour myself a glass of water.

"I don't know, M. I told you before, I don't keep track. Not really."

"What does that mean, 'not really?' That means you do really. Anybody we know? Were they all women, Tom? Were they pretty?"

"No, yes, no." I slip out of my trainers and pull a wad of bills from the toe of each shoe and say in my gameshow host voice, "But get ready, Maggie Pilenski, because you've won a night on the town with your very own private escort!"

She starts crying and walks quickly to her bedroom. We don't go out that night after all. We don't have sex. I try to comfort her and get bored while, for hours, she alternately embraces and shrinks from me. It's gone this way for a few months, and I'm used to it. I lie awake as passing cars stripe the walls of her room with light. I listen to the air conditioner and her wet, hitchy breath as it smoothes and slows in sleep.

I used to tell Maggie the truth when she asked, partly because I thought I owed it to her, and partly because I thought she was interested. "I ravaged five damsels," I'd say in a jolly British accent. "Had my way with a peck of spinsters today, love." I never use the word *rape* when I'm not at work, because really, I don't rape them. It's all arranged ahead of time, pre-paid with a detailed situation, setting, and safety word. On a job, it's a different story. My script is full of it. I throw my voice low and inflate my mild Southie accent to a meanstreets drawl and then I whisper, "Oh fuck, I can't wait to rape you, you slut. I'm going to rape you wicked hard. You won't even be able to walk no more when I'm done raping you." And so forth.

At first, she thought it was cool. Maggie is a performance artist and a waitress and she's smart and has a tongue ring so I figured everything would be fine between us, regarding my job. I told her about it right away, as soon as we started hanging out last year, when I met her after a variety show she was in called "Sluts" where she did a musical number about losing her virginity at sleepaway camp. In the beginning, Maggie asked a lot of questions, sort of like the ones she asks now, but without that savage energy to them. The glint in her eye was a fetching combination of curiosity and lust, and I fell on it and let it feed me.

When I got the job at Dolly's Books, I was really just looking for something retail, something regular. It was two weeks later, when Dolly herself pressed that business card into my hand one night after closing, that I began to consider the odd but subtle goings-on that had been putting me on edge since my first day of work.

"Tom," she said, and her delicate hand hovered above mine a moment before I realized she was dropping something into it. The card was matte black. It felt rubbery to the touch. There was a phone number embossed on one side. That was it.

"What is this?" I asked, flipping the card back and forth as if I expected new, more helpful information to appear on either side.

"Call the number," she said and watched me expectantly.

"Now?" I asked. She shrugged, but didn't turn away, so I walked to the cash register and picked up the phone near it, on the counter.

"No, not on that one. Never that one. Where's your phone?"

I shook my head. I prided myself on not being a tech slave, though the truth was I couldn't really afford a phone. Maggie only rolled her eyes a little whenever I asked to use hers. Dolly frowned. "We'll have to fix that, then."

I was about to get angry. All this mystery—bound up in the small black rectangle I now slid into the back pocket of my jeans—was more annoying than intriguing. It had been a long day, and for the third time this week, one of the other guys I worked with had left in the middle of the shift with some lame excuse, leaving me alone to check out, restock, and lock up. But Dolly put a hand on my neck, and my tension slid away.

"Just call that number when you get home. It might straighten some things out for you." She smiled at me, and my heart beat down in my groin, and I wondered what Dolly would look like naked.

"You're opening tomorrow, right?"

"Yes," I said and watched as she gave me a wink, tossed her long brown hair behind a shoulder and sauntered out the glass doors of the bookstore. So began my marginal life of crime.

As expected, my phone vibrates around 11:30pm. Dispatch text messages me: *cindy. wdner libry 1am. usual.* I disengage myself from a kindly snoring Maggie and message back. I know what Cindy likes, and I have come to Maggie's apartment packed and prepared. Out of my overnight bag, I take a gold chain, a tight black polo shirt and thin, tapered jeans. My loafers are broken in—classic tassels from the 80s—and my feet are comfortable. My package is not. I have to forgo underwear all together—my Levi's are restrictive enough that I'll have to unzip them prematurely, just to allow room for the menacing hard-on it will be my duty to provide for Cindy. I call this my Robert Chambers special, and I usually top it off with some hair gel and a splash of Polo cologne. The finishing touch is the pair of white silk panties in my back pocket.

I slip out silently. I don't want to wake Maggie; she's been so emotional lately. Angry, distant, crying. I feel the first metallic pings of panic begin to straighten my spine. She hadn't touched me in so long, hadn't run her hand over my calves in what seemed like weeks. My calves were her favorite part. "Calf and cock," she would smile and then make a moo sound, followed by a rooster crow and dive her warm face onto my crotch.

I start to stiffen a little beneath the steering wheel, until I remember her this evening, inconsolable and floppy as an infant. When I tried to get her to hold me, her arms went limp and flailed behind my shoulders. Her head rolled on the fine post of her neck as I struggled with her on top of the bed covers. She wouldn't even look me in the eye while I took off my shirt and unzipped my pants. She continued to ignore me, so I shimmied off her cute striped skirt and her panties with the cartoon monkey heads on them, and was pulling her to me by one leg when she began to kick. She sat up and smacked my shoulder and yelled "Fuck!" all at the same time, suddenly skillfully engaged, then scooted up the bed until her back was against the headboard. She continued to not talk but at least she was making eye contact, baleful and shaming. The skin on her ankle was pink and shiny as a sunburn where I'd grabbed her. She would have a bruise there tomorrow. I turned around and lay back into her and she tucked her arms and legs around me like a backpack and we sat that way until she fell asleep with her face pressed into the back of my neck.

I find a pretty good parking space on Quincy Street and walk into the Yard through a small, east gate, one of the few they keep open this late for the night workers. I find the bush where Cindy likes me to lie in wait for her to finish her late night research. She will float down the steps of Widener Library, pretending not to know what's in store for her, or maybe she has really forgotten, just for a moment, the call she'd put in over her dinner break. But no, that's not right, because she'll have been waiting for it, teasing herself with it all afternoon.

The bush I hide in is adjacent to the stone wall behind which I will fuck her with one hand over her mouth, the other squeezing the thin bones of her wrists together. I will jump from behind the bush, I will ask her the time, and when she stops to pantomime checking her watch, I will have her around the throat in an instant, and capture her breast after that.

The hand on her mouth is for show. She never yells—it would draw attention—but makes small suffering noises in the back of her throat until I come or pretend to come, slip my jeans back over my hips, and leave her shiny-eyed on the soft, cedar-chipped ground.

75

I called the number when I got home, the night Dolly slipped the strange black business card into my hand. My apartment then was small and ugly, the front room on the first floor of a dirty, three-story wooden deal that also housed a family of four. I had a private entrance on the side of the building and rarely saw my neighbors, but their children played like marauding elephants overhead every morning. My window overlooked the garbage cans and a lurker's paradise of a dark alley. The street in the front of the house was littered with pubs. Even in the winter, my place was redolent with old diapers and the sounds of violence.

When I dialed the number and waited, I saw spider webs swaying on the walls. My heart beat in my ears, but I knew I wouldn't be long for that dingy place. That card was something special. The telephone slipped a little in my hands, and then that voice, full of cigarettes and whiskey and heaven:

"Hi Thomas, I've been waiting for your call. Welcome to your most dangerous fantasy." She laughed at herself, a little breathy laugh, and continued, "Sorry, that was hammy, I know. Dolly gave me your number. What did she tell you?"

I stammered and blushed. "I, uh...is this a phone sex line?"

She sounded unfazed, expectant, "Kind of. We're a niche pleasure service. Our clientele are mostly women looking for a very specific kind of male company."

"An escort service?" I swallowed hard.

"I guess you could call us that. I know what you mean by

it, and you're right, but we're something...more."

"More?" I squeaked and I cleared my throat.

"Safe Rakes. Cads for Cash. We're still trying to work out our branding. Really, it's best when no one calls us anything. *I* think of us as Safe Rape. That's only in-house though. People generally don't respond well to the word *rape*. Even when it's what they want. See, some women...quite a few it turns out...like their dates a little on the rough side."

"By dates, you mean male prostitutes?"

She laughed again, "You got it. Are you in?"

"Me?" It was some kind of prank. Had to be. Something Dolly whipped up for all her newbies. A test of will and moral fortitude. "Very funny."

"We run a quiet little racket out of the back of the bookstore, me and Dolly. You can call me Dispatch. I hear you are a hottie of the highest degree." She laughed and something in me burned. Was I offended or turned on?

I wasn't vain but I was aware that female attention—a certain crinkle in the eye, a pitch to the voice—had never been very difficult for me to come by. Still, I was living alone, I was broke, I had lately, perhaps, lacked the sort of easy, drunken confidence I had taken for granted in my college years. Dispatch wiggled the bait, and taking one last look around my studio apartment, I knew I was about to jump onto her hook.

"I could call the cops," I said.

"I don't think you will," she whispered.

I smiled into the silent receiver, broad this time, like a shark or a Cheshire cat, about to disappear and reappear as something else entirely. Something a little more dangerous. A little more well-laid. Joke or no, I was ready for it. "Who do you want me to fuck?" I asked.

I check my watch: a fake Rolex with a ticking second hand. Cindy's late, which is not like her. We've been on five or six dates now, and even though I don't know her last name—or even necessarily her first name, since most of our clients don't use their real ones—I do know that she's punctual. This is essential because I'm more and more likely to get arrested the longer I spend squatting out here in the bushes. I'm familiar with the campus police rounds, and really, in this getup and my baby face, I look like any Harvard preppy, but I'd be hard-pressed to explain the lurking aspect of this assignment, which is why I get paid extra for Cindy's particular demands. Usually, I'm out here no more than three or four minutes before she sweeps down the library steps, clutching her research notebooks to her chest, demure to the hilt. But I've been here for almost twenty minutes now, and paranoia's setting in. Plus, I'm beginning to worry about her. I check my phone. Nothing new from Dispatch.

There's a slight commotion somewhere behind me, and I crouch even lower, turn around to assess the danger. Two figures are walking toward me. One, a slight girl with curly brown hair, is weaving a wide path down the sidewalk, probably drunk. She stops twenty feet from my bushes, and turns to yell at the figure approaching behind her. "What the fuck is your problem, motherfucker? I told you, it's over." The motherfucker stalks into view beneath a lamppost. His footsteps carry the uneven weight of the intensely drunk. His face is without expression as he slurs back at her. "Jeeschriss, Laur. Why you gotta go make a scene? I love you, baby. You know I love you. You know that?"

She hisses back at him, arms crossed, wavering a little in place. "You stupid motherfucking douchebag. You fucked her!" Laur starts to cry. "You fucking suck so bad."

Motherfucker moves toward her kind of sideways, and crosses in front of me so that my view of her is blocked completely. All I can see is his huge, lurching form crushing toward her, murmuring quiet incomprehensible things, while she shrills back at him. But suddenly something is happening between the two of them. He jerks back, and then brings his arm up, like he's about to hit her. I didn't know it until

79

this second, but it's exactly what I've been waiting for. I rush out of the bushes, screaming, and go for his knees, drop him easily to the ground. And there's more screaming, from all of us, I think, and a hot tangle of bodies, and I can smell the booze on them. I punch into the mass beneath me, going for the back of his head, making brutal contact, but it's the girl's screams that reach me now and I pull back a little and open my eyes, which I didn't know were closed, and there's Laur on the ground beneath me. I have one second to process the blood on her cheek, the glint of black metal in her hand, and the white pain ripping through my eyes, then I'm on my back, clutching my stabbed face as the blows come quick and fast to my ribs, my chest, the soft give of my stomach. My eyeballs seem to be running down my face. I press my palms to them, willing them back into my head. Then, new voices. More shouting, someone familiar, a soft puff of perfume and Cindy at my ear whispering, "Robert?" as I am hauled up by my armpits and rushed away with my jacket pulled up over my head, like a celebrity trying to evade the paparazzi. In the distance, I hear angry, testicular voices, but can't make them out over the roaring in my ears. Only Cindy, whose arm, I now realize, is hooked into mine, comes through clear.

"What's going on? Did those kids jump you?" A pause and then, "Bert! Bert, come on, let's get him into my car."

There is an answer from behind us, and Cindy's voice again, "No! No cops! Come on, let's just get him out of here." Footsteps come quick, and I cringe as a big palm comes down on my back. "You okay, man? You okay? You okay?" some guy asks over and over, and I feel like a drum kit, a house groove, lost in the throbbing music my body is making until I feel the leather seats beneath me, the comforting sound of a car door slam and the revving pressure pushing me back in my seat as we zoom off into the dark streets of Cambridge.

I feel shrouded, encased. I don't listen to them talk so much as hear them as if from behind a closed door, another room, my hands still pressed to my bleeding eyes like a kid playing peekaboo. The man in the back slowly presses his fingers around my guts, my legs and arms, my head.

"Listen, I really think we should take him to the E.R."

"Bert, no, he can't go to the hospital."

I shake my head and manage a thick, "No hospital."

"What is wrong with you? He's hurt." He tries to move my hands, and I turn toward the window, away from him, as best I can. "Just, at least let me take a look. I'm a doctor." 81

"You have a doctorate in anthropology, Bert." Cindy's scorn is palpable, and I can't help but laugh a little.

"Are you okay? Oh god, Cindy, he's choking." The car

whips to the right then straightens. I imagine Cindy turning back toward us from the driver's seat.

"Okay," I manage. "I'm okay."

Bert's hands have dropped off me. "I took some physical anthropology classes. Through the med school." He's defensive. "Anyway, give me one good reason why we shouldn't go to the hospital."

Cindy's voice is low and immediate. "He's an illegal." She's been cooking this one up. "From Iceland. No green card. He can't take the chance."

"Hospitals can't deny care to—"

"Too big a risk. The Patriot Act." Cindy is firm. Not to be argued with. I've never seen this side of her.

"The Patriot Act? Cin, that's for libraries and—"

"No, Bert. Besides, we're almost to my place."

Bert sighs and touches my hands again. "Robert, just let me see how bad she got you."

I shake my head, gurgle through the tears and blood and snot in my throat, "They'll fall out."

Bert applies more pressure to my wrists, "You've gotta let them breathe. You're holding the pepper spray in. Let your tears work it out. We'll wash them when we get inside."

"Stabbed." I say and lean into the window. The glass is cool on my knuckles, my lower cheek.

"Stabbed? No, she sprayed you. Pepper spray. Here, let me see."

The car stops and Cindy cuts the motor. I almost fall out as she opens my door. "Jesus, okay, let me see." Her hands are cold and strong and they smell like flour. She strokes the backs of my hands and I let a little pressure off my eyes, which seem to be staying in place. She grabs my fingers and squeezes and gently drops them down to my lap.

"Can you open them?" she asks, and I try a little, but the fuzzy streetlight that comes in nearly knocks me over and they close up again. She puts a hand on my head and leads me out of the car with the other. "Watch your head—we're going inside, okay? To my apartment."

I went back to work at the bookstore after talking to Dispatch. She had warned me not to talk to any of the other guys about Safe Rape or I'd be fired immediately. I itched to ask around, but in the end, I was more anxious to get an assignment. I didn't say anything at work, but those sudden workday "emergencies" and last minute shift cancellations that I'd only just begun to notice when Dolly put her card in my hand now seemed to happen all the time. Then one day, after I'd tested clean at a local free clinic (pseudonym: Tad Dangle) and reported back to Dolly, it was my turn. My new phone buzzed and Dispatch's text came through: *323 valentine st. 2pm. victoria. u r caught burglar.*

Victoria lived ten miles west of Boston in one of those doctor's mansions in the suburbs. I went to her door in a ski mask and dressed in black, my heart pounding itself to mush against my ribs. She answered the door and gasped, which I took to be theatrical, so I grabbed her wrist. She immediately snapped out of my grip with a move I remembered from my lifeguarding days, a trick for escaping a drowning person who was dragging you under, which was amazingly close to how I felt. I gulped for air.

"Jesus Christ—I have neighbors, you know. You should always come to the door in jeans and a T-shirt. People will just think you're a student."

"A student?"

"I teach piano." Victoria gestured behind her where the foyer flared into a great room with a wood-beamed ceiling and a baby grand in the corner.

"Oh," I said, and it seemed like I was supposed to say something more. "I played the trombone for two years in high school."

She stepped around me to the windows near the front door. "Where did you park?"

"What?"

"Your car, did you leave it around the block?"

"Oh. Yeah." It hadn't even occurred to me that she would have a driveway. I hadn't been out of the city in a while.

"So you walked around the block in that outfit?" She moaned and put a hand to her head. She was good looking in an older-woman, Sandy-Duncan kind of way.

"I didn't put the mask on until I got to the door," I said. "Besides, it's winter. People wear ski masks in the winter."

"Not in Newton." She pursed her lips and reached into her pocket, "Look, here's your script." I took the piece of paper she handed me. My parts were highlighted in yellow. "Now go upstairs. I'm going to arrive home 'unexpectedly.'" She air-quoted the word *unexpectedly*. I wondered how I was ever going to get hard for this woman. "Okay? Then you come downstairs and 'surprise' me, and then we go into the script."

Victoria's bedroom was large and vaguely masculine and filled with photos in severe wooden frames. There were a lot of her and some older guy who was probably her husband. You didn't get wood-beam ceilings and baby grands from teaching piano. There were pictures of them on the top of a green mountain; in visors and zinced noses on a yacht with a caught swordfish hanging behind them; on skis in front of a European-looking chalet. I heard the front door open,

85

and I imagined Victoria standing inside the hall, calculating the angle she could open the door—wide enough to sound convincing, as if she has just come in from outside, but not too wide, which might alert her neighbors to the fishy goings-on. I could practically hear her counting to five in her head. Then the front door closed and her voice rang out quite naturally, "Anybody home? John?" That wasn't in my script, which I'd memorized quickly, all five lines of it. Already, she was improvising. I walked quietly down the hall to the stairs, which I began to creep down. I was only to the landing when she walked into the hallway and did a double take, as if I'd caught her eye unexpectedly. Then she screamed—loud enough to raise the hair on my neck, but not so loud that it would be heard in this neighborhood, where the houses were set affluently apart. Her eyes went wide and she stumbled backwards, reaching for the wall. It was an impressive performance.

"Shut the fuck up. Where's the jewels?" I growled, advancing down the stairs.

"I...I don't know what you're talking about," she said with wide, wet eyes.

"The jewels. I know they're here, bitch. If you don't give 'em to me, you're going to be sorry." I wondered where she got this stupid dialogue. At least she was convincing. She'd nearly got me believing it was real.

"Oh god, please don't hurt me!" She began to cry what looked like real tears, and suddenly something switched on inside of me.

"I fucking warned you, cunt." I ad-libbed and rushed toward her, grabbed her by the neck. I wanted to stuff my dick into that whining, begging mouth. I wanted to shut her up, make her take it. I was already stiff. I ripped her shirt from the collar. A shoulder pad flopped toward me, over her stomach. I jerked her bra down so it tangled with the shirt at her waist. She looked ridiculous and genuinely frightened and this kept me going as I pushed her down on the staircase, tore off her pants and her big underwear, and fucked her from behind, grunting out loud and swearing even though I'd always been very quiet during sex.

Cindy brings another cold washcloth for my pepper-sprayed eyes. Somehow, she's convinced Bert to leave without calling the paramedics or the police. She sits on her couch, near my feet. Even though we've had sex a few times, there's something inappropriately intimate about how the cushions jiggle me into her. Neither one of us talks for awhile, and somehow that feels okay. Finally, Cindy says, "Sorry about that, back there. I was a little late for our appointment and then I ran into Bert, who insisted on walking me across the Yard. He made some excuse about how he's heard that rape incidents have doubled in Cambridge in the last two years." I try not to laugh and end up sucking painfully through the raw, chemical tunnel of my throat.

"It's not funny," Cindy says.

"I was choking."

"So that's my story tonight. What's yours?"

"Can you have normal sex?" I wonder aloud. I don't know where I'm going with this. It seems easier to say whatever I want when I can't see anything, when there's a wet washcloth splayed like a jellyfish across my stinging face.

"Can you?" she says

"Can you?" I ask again.

"Canoe," she says and slides her hands all around under my shirt.

"Kayak."

"Tug." She unzips my pants and fishes around in my boxers' gap for my softie.

"Steamboat Willy," I answer. This makes her laugh a breeze as she puts her mouth on me. Her lips slide up and down my dick. Cock, I correct in my head. Maggie claims that once it's hard, it's properly referred to as a cock. Maggie. My stomach thunders at the thought of her, at how I'm about to cheat on her for real, about to have sex outside of our agreement (only for pay, and only clients of Safe Rape and only when the two intersect) and the thought of it is breaking my own heart, suddenly, before I even have a chance to start on Maggie's.

I take the washcloth off my face and look down at Cindy between my legs. Her eyes are vulnerable and expectant. My hands come down on her head and she gags as my cock hits the back of her throat. She tries to come up but I keep her there. I say, "Take it all, bitch," and her hands grab onto my wrists and try to pry them off, but I'm stronger than she is, so she screams, a strangled burble, wet against me. I take the pressure off and she jumps up, sputtering.

"What the fuck?" she coughs.

"Where's the jewels?" It's the first thing that pops into my head. "Give me the jewels or I'm gonna ream you until my cum is spurting out your ears."

Cindy backs away, one hand at her throat. "Stop it. We're not playing now."

"You think this is a game?" I yell, my erection deflating. "Give me the money or you'll wish you were never born."

"Be quiet!" she hisses, "My walls are thin. The neighbors—"

"Isn't this what you want, you slut? For me to stick my

89

dick in your dirty hole?"

Cindy winces and goes to the kitchen. I zip up my pants and tuck in my polo shirt, which is dusty and ripped. She stands at the sink, chugging a glass of water as her red eyes dart from me to the floor.

"We had an appointment."

She swallows and sets the glass in the sink. "Not anymore. Not since I saved you getting your ass kicked by those drunk kids. You ruined it. Get out of here."

"I could rape you for real." I say. This has never occurred to me before, and it's not like I'm going to, but it's true.

"Anybody could, shithead," she says.

And this is also true.

I have to get home to Maggie. I have to tell her I'm not going to do this anymore. I have to tell her to be careful. That the whole world is full of thrusting cocks. I'll pay for karate classes or judo—whatever's the most lethal. I'll give her rides to and from work. We'll put a deadbolt on her door. She'll have the loudest whistle in all of Boston, pepper spray, a knife.

My phone. It's Dispatch, probably calling to fire me. Better to get this done now. I answer the call.

"Tom," she purrs. "Sorry to call so late. We have a job for you, but I wanted to make sure you were available before

I put it through." She doesn't mention the Yard or Cindy, and she definitely hasn't fired me on the spot.

"You're right, D, it's late, and I'm on my way home, and I don't think I'm going to do this anymore."

"Really?" she asks, though she doesn't sound surprised. "How about just one more job tonight and we'll have a talk about it tomorrow?"

"No," I say, "I'm done."

"Sorry, Tom, one more job tonight. I'm not asking. I caught wind of an interesting story the Harvard cops might want to hear—something about the assault of a freshman girl in the Yard? Might be the same guy who sexually assaulted a research assistant at her apartment earlier tonight."

"Fuck you."

"We'll talk tomorrow. Job's coming through," she says and hangs up.

The text message tells me the job is at a pier in Southie. My balls tell me they're in a vise. Client is a stranded motorist. I take the first U-turn I can and pull over because I think I'm going to throw up. My stomach settles and I call Maggie, but she's sleeping and doesn't answer. I mean to tell her I love her and that I will be home soon, but instead I say, "I'm sorry," to her voicemail and quickly hang up.

There's no traffic downtown this time of night, not even

at the harbor. It's all tourist restaurants and condos these days, the big fishing boats have moved south to New Bedford and out to the Cape. Even the old Combat Zone is quiet now. I turn onto Summer, then D. There's not a single prostitute out, except me. I park and take a nice long walk to the pier, hoping it will clear my head. I try to keep in the shadows of the processing plants and warehouses. I see the car up ahead and try to wipe my eyes into focus as they tear and sting, acting up again in the sea wind. It's an old Celica and even though the sodium lamp across the street gives everything a dirty-orange cast, I know it's blue. I know the bumper sticker will read "Beauty School Dropout." I know Led Zeppelin's *IV* is on the tape deck, stuck there since Maggie bought the car for three hundred dollars from a graduating MassArt student three years ago.

Her window is already open when I jog up to it.

"What are you doing out here? This is dangerous."

Maggie looks up at me and clears her throat, "Oh, thank god. My car broke down. The engine won't start."

"That's because it's a piece of shit. You shouldn't be out here."

"Well, good thing for the kindness of strangers. Do you know anything about cars? Do you think you could take a look at it?" Her eyes are fierce, defiant.

"Maggie, why are you out here?"

"You must have me confused with someone else. I'm Patricia," she extends her hand and I push it gently away.

"Stop it. My car's here. Let's go home."

"I don't think that's a good idea. I don't even know you. You could be a serial killer or a mad rapist."

"Not tonight." I open her door. "Come on."

"No!" she yells and her face falls into itself. "*You* come on. I want you to do it to me."

"Do what?" I say and crouch down before her, wincing from my bruises. She puts a hand in my hair and pulls my head forward hard and whispers in my ear, "Rape me." I try to pull back, but now she's got the other hand on my balls and is squeezing and dragging me on top of her into the car. "Rape me, asshole." She knocks the wind out of herself on the gearshift, and her grip lets up enough for me to slide back out of the car.

"Maggie," I beg. She reclines back and the lines of her blur as my eyes fill up.

"Or I'll lie here until somebody does it for real."

She unzips her jeans and tugs them down around her thighs and turns her head into the passenger side seatback, closes her eyes. The ring of a buoy comes off the water as the wind shifts, raising goose bumps on her stomach and legs. She doesn't move.

I don't even notice that I've already taken my cock in my hand as tears and snot glaze my face and I blubber, "Okay. Okay, I'll try."

THE FAT OF THE LAND

After twelve years out east, you're moving home. Friends can't believe you'd trade Manhattan for Iowa. You tell them, imagine living in a small, dirty box. The garbage bins parked just outside your windows keep you from opening them, so your mattress smells of the garlic you cook with. Now imagine that once a month, half of your paycheck goes to the owner of the small, dirty box. Life outside the box is beautiful and exciting but you are allowed only a whiff, now and then, of this life—just enough to make you desperate for it.

In New York, you feel tough. You walk fast and sharp down the street. Your feet are calloused, your legs sinewy. You walk to work and the park. You walk to museums and clubs. On your lunch hour, you walk to the Flatiron Building just because you realize one day you've never seen it in person. You walk up and down the Hudson eating your lo mein lunch as you go.

But once you're in Iowa, you buy a car. You resist at first, but soon it will be fall and your bicycle is kind of shitty, and you borrowed it from a friend of a friend who is making noise about wanting it back. He's afraid it will be stolen or vandalized—common in a college town like this—and has made it clear that if this happens, you'll be asked to buy a new bike for him, which would be very expensive. You realize borrowing a bike is a little like renting an apartment: everything depends on whether or not you're dealing with an asshole. Since you're not sure, you buy a car.

The car is used, but the price of it still takes your breath away. It's the first car you've ever bought for yourself and the most expensive thing you've ever owned. Besides the initial cost, there are oil changes, insurance, tire care, and gas. The expenses feel decadent, which soothes you. New Yorkers are into decadence, you tell yourself, and what is more decadent to a New Yorker than a car?

You get a job writing standardized tests. On your first lunch break at the new job, you go out the back door of the office building but there is nowhere to walk. You are surrounded by warehouses and semis. No sidewalks, just paved drives for loading and unloading. You go back inside and read *The New York Times* online for the rest of your lunch hour.

Every Sunday, you go to your mother and stepfather's house for family dinner. Your stepfather's a very good cook. You eat plates of pasta with three kinds of sauce (pesto, alfredo, marinara: the Italian flag). You eat Ritz crackers heaped with local blue cheese and dumplings dripping with beefy, salty lobster sauce. You drink half a bottle of table wine. When anyone asks you how work is, you say, "Testy," and they always laugh because that's how much they love you.

After you've been back a couple of months, you find an email from Seth in an old account you hardly ever check. It's dated three weeks ago and reads,

I own a restaurant now.
You should stop by.
—S

This is typical of Seth: an invitation to a public space. Something special out of nothing. It's not exactly a date, but you don't have anything else to do, so one day after work, you go.

It's a barbecue restaurant and before you even make it in the door, the smell has you; the woodsmoke makes you nostalgic for someone else's Midwestern childhood. Seth is standing behind the register in a yellow apron and a T-shirt. For someone who cooks for a living, you can't believe how thin he is. You haven't seen each other in fifteen years. He was pudgy when he was your high school boyfriend—that succulent baby fat. He comes out from around the counter

99

and gives you a spidery hug. In his embrace, the smoke smell is overwhelming, as if he is the one scenting the restaurant instead of the other way around.

He takes you through the swinging double doors to the kitchen and shows you the smoker—biggest in the state, special ordered. Back at the front of the house, he points out each handblown glass sconce, the distressed brick walls, the enormous dining room windows—garage doors when the place was a gas station, before he converted it. Then, he waves a hand at the woodburnt menu and asks what you want to eat. Something catches your eye and you say, "What's a *Good Lord*?"

"That," he says, "is my invention. Four of God's greatest foods on one bun—a burger topped with a pork tenderloin topped with bacon topped with cheese."

You make a sound in the back of your throat that's meant to convey disgust.

"Yeah, it's awesome," he says. "I'll make two."

A few minutes later, Seth sets the basket in front of you. The sandwiches are so tall and wide. Your mouth will never fit around them. You're about to ask him what you should do when he squishes one sandwich down with the heel of his hand. Bacon crackles under his palm and cheddar sweats out. "You have to smash them down, really make them yours."

Seth motions to you and you squish the other one so it's as squat as the first. "I put some mayo on there for you. It's not a real Good Lord without mayo."

Your heart pounds. You take a bite and sigh into the slippery, salty wonder of it. Seth's watching for your reaction. He looks like his old teenage self. You swallow and smile and hoist the abomination triumphantly into the air. He smiles, relieved, and goes back into the kitchen. A few minutes later, the front door chimes when the only other customer in the place leaves. Seth comes through the double doors again, already taking off his apron. "Hey, there's no one here. You want to fuck in the walk-in?"

You're still formulating a response when he takes your hand and leads you through the pantry. Large, earthy lettuce heads are scattered on the ground, tumbled from their cartons. Great vats of Sysco fryer oil and enormous cans of kidney beans make you feel small, childlike, as if you are playing in the kitchen of a giant. Seth leaves the door of the giant fridge open a crack in case of customers. "You still have that great, big ass?" he asks and gently takes down your pants, bends you over. He is delicate while he looks at it and then, suddenly, he is not delicate at all. You clutch at a full rack of ribs as he pushes you against the shelving and you realize that you're still holding your first Good Lord. You put it down next to the ribs as he pulls out and comes, moaning. He gives you a kiss on the neck as you both button your jeans and you're sixteen again. In the dining room, you eat the second Good Lord and are pink and slightly breathless for the rest of the day.

It takes you awhile to figure out that you've outgrown your pants. It's still mostly warm, so you're wearing a lot of skirts and hardly notice when, now and then, a pair gets stuck at your thighs. You write it off as dryer shrinkage. You've never been skilled at laundry. In New York, you always sent your clothes out—laundry service being one of the three things cheaper in New York than everywhere else (the other two: cabs and cut flowers). But when you try on some jeans you find stuffed in the back of your closet—unwashed since the move—you finally discover the truth. You've grown. You dig out the rest of your fall and winter pants and try on each pair. Nothing fits. Your belly—where did it come from?—hangs out over the top of the waistbands in the puffy style your sister calls a muffin top. The zippers stop halfway up, stubborn. The button tabs reach for each other and miss by a mile, clumsy acrobats across the pale expanse of your hips. You buy a scale at Wal-Mart. You've gained nineteen pounds in two months. You're not really sure how this went so remarkably unnoticed.

You've just hit Seth's vaporizer when the doorbell rings, which sends you into a coughing fit. Seth goes to the door and when he returns, he drops a pizza box on the table between you and opens it—the pizza is covered in ham and pineapple and it's Chicago style, which means instead of a thick dough base, there's mostly just cheese. Pounds of it.

"You ever had a Hawaiian?"

You shake your head and make a face. "Is that what you ordered? It's really…" Your face feels somehow not part of the rest of your head. It's been a long time since you got high. You smile and that seems to help unite your head and face.

Seth's eyes are red and full and a little squinty. He picks up a piece of pizza and holds it out to you. "You will eat this and like it."

"It's really…tropical." You remain unconvinced but you take the heavy piece from him anyway and put it in your mouth. The pineapple bursts against your tongue and sets off the saltiness of the ham. When you open your eyes, Seth is working on his own piece, smiling his I-told-you-so.

"What? Everything tastes good when you're stoned." You finish a slice and when you toss him your crust, he pockets it in a cheek and takes another hit. Then you're following him to the couch, and he's kissing you, deep, becrumbed and slobbery. You think to yourself, it's as if he's trying to eat my tongue, and because you're stoned, for a second you panic and pull back. But he moves his mouth to your neck and that feels good, his hands clutching the more of you there is now. Ten minutes later and he's done his good work for the both of you. You get to thinking before you fall asleep like this—him on top, giant TV screen still aglow—that his lesser weight pressing you feels like love. The next day, you reheat a slice of the pizza in the microwave at work and eat it at your desk. You close your eyes and chew, feeling dizzy, something warm rising in you like bread.

One day, you're able to pay off all your outstanding urban debt. A knot inside you releases, a knot you'd forgotten was there. You make a promise to yourself to spend wisely, but you save one low-interest credit card from some internet place called Land's Bank. Your friend from high school, Cate, whom you meet once a week for martinis, refers to this credit card as "the fat of the land" because you have, so far, charged two gym memberships; four diet cookbooks; yoga classes; special massages that claim to break up fat deposits, which are then supposedly flushed from your system when you pee; and a diet drug that binds the fat you eat and passes it undigested. One of the side effects of the drug is that it may cause you to shit yourself. You bring an extra pair of pants to work and then stop taking the drug when you realize what you're preparing for. In New York, you spent your money on books and plays, sometimes unable to buy groceries for a week after. Where else could you live on air? You don't miss it much, though perhaps you have now overcorrected a bit too far in the opposite direction. Weeks pass in a drowse. You've adapted to Seth's odd restaurant hours, and of course you still have your own job to which you show up late and fuzzy. Instead of hitting the gym, you buy longer skirts, which have fortuitously come back into fashion this year. You pack away your shorts and minis in large Tupperware tubs. Though still warm, it's actually fall anyway—what the farmers call an Indian summer. They predict it will break very soon.

By January, you've grown your winter coat—a layer of fat that covers your body from elbows to knees like a quilt. You feel tucked in for the season. When the cold comes in earnest, Seth's restaurant is the only place you go. There's always a beer waiting at your table and you know better than to order from the menu. After he hugs you hello, Seth disappears into the back and returns with red plastic baskets stacked up his arms. You pluck them off as he narrates: "Smoked duck, lamb burger, batter-fried Oreos." Then he sits across from you and watches you eat. He doesn't talk but his knobby knees press into yours and his sharp, serious gaze makes you slightly nervous and very horny. When you're stuffed, the button on your jeans undone, your food baby patted, he kisses your cheek, the smoke and oil and sweat coming off of him like a secret you share. He pauses in the kiss and you press your tongue to his neck soft and fast, an amuse-bouche, a quick taste before he runs back to the kitchen.

In February, your ex calls you from New York and cries. His cat, Sontag, has died, and the interim grief has convinced him that allowing you to leave was the worst mistake of his life. He thinks his nicest feature is his hands, and so adorns them with rings. Over the line, you can hear him clicking them together. You tell him you live in Iowa now. You're not home on holiday break. You have a job and—and here you almost say "boyfriend" but stop yourself and smile—responsibilities and if he wants to talk about amends, he's going to have to come out here to do it. There is a long silence, at the end of which he politely declines, every trace of teary regret gone from his voice.

106

The next morning, you're driving to work, taking the slightly longer way past Seth's house. You are absently smiling to yourself as you cross the intersection to his block until you see a girl standing on his front porch smoking a cigarette. It's freezing outside and not an inch of her is visible besides her black hair—scarf to her eyes, parka to the knees, thick red mittens and bright orange moon boots. Something tings in your stomach and you make a U-turn at the end of the block but when you pass by again, she's disappeared.

You don't know what to think or do about this, so you act like nothing has happened. The following night, you're sucking the last tendrils of meat off a rib bone at the restaurant, looking absentmindedly out the window at the pedestrians shuffling by on the icy sidewalks, when someone is suddenly standing beside your booth, peering down at you, angry. Startled, you practically inhale the bone in your hand as you turn and see a young, lovely Indian girl—she can't be more than twenty-two—glaring at you from above. When you make eye contact, she begins to scream so fiercely her words are unrecognizable as words. When she steps back, you see her orange boots and slowly, as if someone is adjusting a radio tuner, her words start to make sense. You don't wish to repeat them. And then Seth is there, picking up the girl by the waist and pulling her away from you. She doesn't even seem to notice that her boots are a foot off the floor. She squirms and flails her limbs as if she would drag you to hell if she could. Her tirade continues as Seth maneuvers her out the door and puts her down in the parking lot. Once outside, the girl doesn't stop to take a breath, but seamlessly turns her attention to Seth and continues to yell. He yells back. Like everyone else in the place, you're turned around in your booth, watching this through the giant windows. You can't tell what they're saying to each other, but the girl takes off around the corner and is gone. You're amazed at her fleetness on the ice.

When you realize you're holding the rib bone in front of you, defensively, you drop it on the floor and rise from your booth. Seth comes back into the restaurant but rushes into the kitchen, brushing by you without a glance. You keep going, out to the parking lot, which still seems to hum with their fight. On the drive home, even while your stomach is twisting and seething, you can't help but wonder if that reed of a girl is a vegetarian. Of all your unanswered questions, this one—which makes you a racist as well as a sucker—is the one that breaks you down.

Seth calls and calls but leaves no messages. He slow smokes ribeyes and deposits them, rare, in your mailbox, with instructions for how to cook them down to medium rare in your oven.

You decide to go on a date with someone Cate describes as "a grown-up." This is meant as a friendly rib at your taste in men. Allen is a tax attorney with broad shoulders. He really likes U2. Cate reports these things over martinis as if you have a list and are making check marks in little boxes as she speaks.

This U2 thing has been an odd theme shared by many of your boyfriends: at least four of them have loved U2 beyond reason or shame. It's always embarrassed you a little, and long ago, you'd taken pains to scrub the band from your collection. But these men you date are insatiable for the stadium shows; the pay-per-view European concerts; the 3-D, interactive, Save Africa, internet happenings. It's a common thread you've pondered before. It means something, you're sure, but what? Over your first dinner, emboldened by two glasses of wine and a flirty conversation, you ask Allen.

"So, Cate tells me you like U2. What is it about them? A lot of people—guys I know—really, really love U2," you say after you've swallowed a rubbery bit of fettuccine. Immediately, your face gets warm because the tone of your voice is kind of snobby even though you'd tried very hard to sound insincerely nonjudgmental.

"What do you mean?" Allen is suspicious.

"Um. I mean...is it a guy thing? Like Rush? What's so great about them?"

Allen frowns and puts his full fork down. "I guess I

don't know what you're getting at. They make great music. They stand for change in the world, change for the better. Their songs are touching and about something." His face has become a bit red and your stomach feels heavy, overfull. He continues, sharp: "I guess they're not really cool, right?"

You sink back in your seat, surprised by the counterattack, and take a sip of water to buy yourself a second. "Oh…U2's cool?" you say and wish that you could die.

"People our age who think they know what's cool are usually underemployed pricks who take handouts from their parents, people who should probably realize that getting a life is," he makes air quotes, "'what's cool.' Anyway," Allen stabs at his dinner, before giving a soft, forced laugh. "Anyway, sorry. I just hate that stuff. That fake artistic posturing. I get a little defensive sometimes. Who cares about all that anyway?"

You smile and nod your head and feel like a jerk because you will be relating this story to Cate, word for word, later tonight, when you're in bed alone, and your laughter then will make up for your discomfort now, at least until Cate says, "Well…who does care? He's a really nice guy, you know." And you'll be ashamed of yourself and agree to another date, and then another.

Weekends with Allen. You wake up with "The Unforgettable Fire" on repeat in your brain. Once, you call him Al and he corrects you: Allen. The first time you spend the night together, you kneel above him, and peel off your shirt in a manner you hope is seductive and intense. He clears his throat and turns off the light, handles you hard, like a basketball. You wilt a little and then get used to it.

Allen thinks eating out is a waste of money. He runs, and cooks little, eats cereal for dinner and steamed chicken before the charity half-marathons that loop around town in the spring. You learn how to prepare quinoa and eat it out of bowls on his sticky leather couch. He asks you to run with him and sometimes you do, though you never get the hang of it. Your body can't find the rhythm and your shins scream for days after. It strikes you as a man's sport. Your breasts and ass and thighs bounce and chafe. You always finish walking, Allen out ahead of you on the rain-slicked sidewalks, chugging along like something built from a single block of material.

When you find a top sirloin wrapped in foil and stuffed between your screen and front doors, you take it to the food bank and burn the note in your sink without reading it.

Weeks pass, months. You are shrinking. Your ass deflates like it has sprung a slow leak and you need to wear belts to keep your fat pants up, then your skinny ones. Allen starts leaving the lights on when you have sex.

One night, he takes you out to dinner to celebrate—tax season has wrapped and he's made partner at work. The place he takes you has candles and cloth napkins and an Italian name even though the owners are Lutherans from Minnesota. The waiters wear bow ties and white towels over their arms. Every entrée has twenty ingredients. You're tired and not especially hungry. When the waiter arrives, Allen orders while you glance around the dining room—the paintings on the wall are abstract and in the same pastel palette as the curtains. The waiter leaves before you have a chance to speak.

You stare after him for a moment and turn to Allen. "Did you just order for me?" you ask.

"Don't worry—I know what's good here. You'll love it." Allen nods approvingly, at nothing. "Isn't this a nice place?"

Something you've learned about lawyers is that they ask rhetorical questions in order to change the subject. You want to tell him that this isn't a rhetorical question, exactly. That, to some people, this is a nice place. A place with prominent street parking in front, so that anyone in town who drives by can see where you're dining. A nice, bland, Midwestern version of class. You sigh and feel guilty for your grumpiness and try to listen attentively while he talks about clients and his new responsibilities at work.

Your food arrives—a poached filet of sole dripping on

112

a bed of rosemary and surrounded by the artful squiggles of some sort of lemon sauce. Allen's chicken is roasted and pilafed. He pushes it to the side and cuts the sole into pieces in front of you. He tells you he loves you and moves to feed you a bite, leaning over the table, mauve cloth napkin held below the fork to catch the warm water that drips from it. You smile hard and put your mouth around the fork. Your lips are dry and the fork catches on the top one when he pulls it back, taking a tiny bit of skin with it. It only stings a little, but you feel you might cry where you sit. With a hand over your mouth, you toss your napkin on your chair and walk quickly toward the back of the restaurant where you sense the bathroom must be.

By the kitchen, you notice a wine chiller, full of ice, on a cart, waiting to be wheeled into the dining room. The waiter gives you an expectant smile as he places a bottle of champagne in it.

The fish rolls off your tongue into the stainless-steel garbage can. You rinse your mouth with water from the tap. You push into a stall. Your nice crepe pants—the ones you'd bought for your new, smaller body—make a shushing sound as they settle against the immaculate toilet seat. You stare into the faux-marble stall door and wonder how you will ever make it to dessert.

HISTOLOGY

{the study of the microscopic (structure of tissues)}

Fig. 5

Fig. 15

Fig. 13

Fig. 14

Fig. 7

Fig. 8

Fig. 9

Fig. 10

Fig. 11

Fig. 12

Fig. 4

Fig. 1

PEST

A scratching and the singing of light through a million filaments, a brilliant stench and the peck of these feet. Haunch high, it is not a slink so much as a hump. Here, in stump, we say, where you come from now? Was in stump, we say. Is when we are in stump that such happens. Wo's why we in stump to begin. Some in stump and some out in form. Twos or so in stump, but in form: all, noses raising fog. We smell each and each and each. All eaches snuck round, round our haunches, we hidle with all. Here, who in stump? We are. We sleep. With eaches in stump, we sleep. But there in mid, up a bit, the scree of kit or mate. We all take up the scree, a nerve like that run haunch to haunch to haunch. The form a racking-thing when scree it spread. What it done? What it done? Some glass-eye-no-scree ask us all in form, but what we do? We scree. The nerve it follow form, no choice in us, no choice of choice. We are stump and form all, and when scree run through, it thread out up and down and stump to stump, a split crack, and shake the nest of nests. Crier finds the thread and winch it back to us: in stump got cracked and shaked, and we snatched out. We who was up in stump last when they big crawlers tore the stone of ground and spit chaff and grain. We in stump take, then put deep in the nest of nests. Where we were, there were we, in form, but short some. The scree went small but we crowded in to fill the hole in form with us. Kit or mate, we say, take us haunch and haunch, and be whole, be form, be here. No scree. And when the warm come more and touch each tail and claw, we all—form and stump, eaters, growlers, takers, biters—we see in warm the form of us complete. No hole, no scree. This thumby pound, just hearts.

FULL

We are worrying about that job, the one two thousand miles away, in a desolate rural corner, and whether or not our love will survive the distance year. We are thinking of all that cheap real estate. We are wondering whether we are good enough for that job, whether our resume is voluptuous and shapely or overstuffed. We worry that we binge on praise and starve without it. We sometimes think of our dogs and how one of them seems not to eat enough and the other, too much. We worry that one day the dogs might eat the rabbit we took in after a sister's divorce. We keep them separate with a complex system of baby gates, but we know accidents happen. We try to be vigilant.

We let our guard down, sometimes, and think of the people who have hurt us, who are unlikely to apologize. We remember the restaurants they worked in, the way we would hang out in the booth near the pinball machine, waiting for a busied glance, a nod, a free plate of cheese sticks that could be read like tea leaves: a good and generous mood. We worry that our pride prevents us from apologizing to the people we hurt, but it's not like we lose sleep over it. We wonder if one of us drinks too much and possibly lies about it, but it's not like we lose sleep over it. We feel the weight of winter in our flesh, in the coy way it bunches out over the tops of our jeans. We worry we are not having sex enough, that desire has become buried, like the lawn under the clouds, the particulate compound in our air, the snow. We cannot eat enough soup: broccoli cheddar, tomato bisque. We are never full.

We remember when we did not work so much, when our work was not so important. We hope our co-workers like us and say nice things about us when we aren't around, and on the way to work we buy expensive donuts with the thought of winning them over. We pretend this is generosity. We worry that we are not generous to anyone, to each other. We sometimes feel our generous hearts cooking down to a stiff syrup. We wonder when we will disappoint each other. We wonder how. We think about the ways we might disappoint each other like flavors of rancid ice cream in a polished steel freezer.

We wake sometimes in the night, frightened and staring into faces we don't recognize, and rest hands on each other's flanks until the feeling passes. It passes when we remember the bread we baked earlier, our hands braiding the dough like the hair of a farmgirl, our hands crossing until we could not distinguish what was yours from what was mine.

CORRIDORS

The man and the woman were not on vacation. They were just headed upstate for the weekend to pretend as though the house that belonged to the man's parents, who were in Hawaii, was theirs. They couldn't afford a real vacation, so they started conversations they knew would lead to arguments, conversations that began, "Why did you...?" and "Why don't you...?" and ended with sounds in place of words. The man tended toward a dry snuffling and the woman understood the most inappropriate moments to laugh. When they reached the house, they moved, as if synchronized, to bedrooms on different floors.

The man and the woman both kept things from each other. Not the things you'd think, but small, bloodless accomplishments. The man did not know the woman had been slightly famous in her town, as a child, for proposing a bill that required antifreeze to be treated with an embittering agent to make it unappetizing to pets and children. The woman didn't know the man had once been an excellent cross-stitcher. It was how they remembered themselves when they were dug deep inside each other.

The television set had been shamed to the guest room in the basement, which was where the woman had set her bag and was now bent over the book she was pretending to read. The man came down and turned on the television, fiddled with the cable, snuffled. The woman sighed her way out of the room and up two flights in search of a bathtub. She ran the water until it lost heat, entombed herself, and began to read in earnest. Eventually, the man's voice found her locked door and asked if she wanted Chinese. She thought the fetal thrumming of the water in the room might have softened him. She liked the way he sounded through the layers of wood and drywall—distant and slightly worried, busied at getting them fed. She understood that this was how one person lived with another for decades—apart and echoing at each other through fiberglass and thumping pipes, voices bending around the angled ends of so many corridors.

PASSIVE-AGGRESSIVE

X: I will not speak to you because I am deeply hurt that you have not yet volunteered to watch my dog while I am on vacation with my girlfriends in Las Vegas.

Y: I will not volunteer to look after your dog for you while you are in Las Vegas, not because I don't love you, but because I wish to express my disapproval of your trip to Las Vegas with your girlfriends. I don't want you to go to Las Vegas because you may be hit on by drunk men and possibly have sex with one or more of them.

X: I will not speak about my anger over the dog because it would sound trite, even though I do believe it possibly reveals deeper and larger problems in our relationship. Instead, I will tell you, once again, that I think it's time for you to get a job, and/or possibly begin taking anti-depressants, and/or see a therapist.

Y: I will not respond to your request that I get a job and/or possibly begin taking anti-depressants and/or see a therapist, because I am right now imagining a drunk man in a white baseball cap sipping from a large plastic cocktail cup shaped like the Eiffel Tower as he enters you from behind. To displace this image, I will now turn on the television and begin flipping through the channels.

X: I will assume that your silence means you are not interested in gainful employment or your own mental health. Conventional wisdom about such disinterest also points to the possibility that you may not be capable of loving me in your current condition, a theory that may take as supporting evidence your lack of interest in caring for my dog while I am in Las Vegas with my girlfriends. I will not ask another question of you this evening because I am feeling a mixture of emotions that include an exhausting mélange of self-pity, self-loathing, and the usual generalized rage that I will perhaps turn outward toward you when I have more energy. Possibly tomorrow morning.

Y: I will not speak to you because I have found out, rather fortuitously, that there is a mini-marathon of *The Office* being broadcast on cable right now. I can see from the close-up shot of a bat hanging from the ceiling of the eponymous office that the episode playing at this very moment is "Business School." Originally broadcast in season three (2007-2008), "Business School" is, indeed, one of my favorite episodes. I do not notice that you have left the room, although, at commercial break, I will hear you making a small noise in the bedroom and assume that you are talking to your dog, or with your girlfriends about all the sex with strangers you may or may not have in Las Vegas, and not that you are crying quietly, facing the wall, waiting to shudder away from me when I come to bed, finally, many hours from now.

THE LAST NIGHT THEY
SPENT TOGETHER
BEFORE THE SEPARATION

They put the children to bed, all eight of them. They put the camera crew members to bed, all eight of them, though most of the crew stayed up, listening through the thin suburban floors, clutching their fists at each other for all that was not being recorded.

In the kitchen, she said to him, "You may not agree, but the children really are the most important thing. We have to think of them in all of this." He said to her, "I know." Then he said, "You don't have to be such a bitch about it." She said, "Is that the way you talk to the mother of your children?" and he said, "Stop thinking of the children. Just for a minute, can't you think of us?"

She did not storm away into another room, because she could feel the camera crew listening, and even though they were each tucked into beds in the bunking area behind the false wall in the basement, and their cameras were not on, she felt beholden to them, like a child to its teachers. Instead of storming away, she took a bag of apples, provided by Dole, and began to slice them for the children's lunches. Thus, she was in a position to dramatically thrust the knife into the air when he made his next remark, which he delivered as if it were scripted, though that was not strictly allowed:

"I think I'm in love with someone else."

125

There was the satisfying thunk as the knife became a heavier weight in her hand and torpedoed, as if by destiny, into the heavy wood cutting board in front of her. She thought to herself, "Cut." She may have actually said, "Cut." And then an uncertain silence fell between them because what more was there to do or say?

He had backed up against the refrigerator when the knife came down, as if he'd been commanded to wince, though he knew exactly where that knife would go and that it would stay there. This was not Court TV. He stood in a small avalanche of happy drawings of houses and stick mommies and daddies and finger-painted abstractions that he was almost certain had not been made by his own children but by the children of his producers and editors and, it was rumored, perhaps by the extremely gifted two-year-old daughter of one of the network executives, a toddler with a prodigious understanding of light and color and space, drawings that had come down when he had backed himself without fear against the refrigerator door while her knife came to rest in the place that it had to.

So she moved to him. And now he did wince because it was not something he understood. Her mouth was doing that slight twitching thing it did, which could mean she was annoyed or about to laugh or possibly that she was having an allergic reaction to the heavy foundation she wore so her skin would appear skin-colored on television. He wasn't sure anymore. He wasn't sure he had ever been sure. He might watch old episodes in his new bachelor pad to see if there was something recognizable about the way her mouth moved in the first season. Or perhaps it was a tic she had picked up for the cameras. He would go back and watch all the seasons to see what fragments of his wife revealed themselves, and build a montage of her, something that would finally make sense.

So she moved to him and put her mouth to his neck. Then his jaw, just below the left earlobe. Then the earlobe.

The camera crew, highly trained in their field, heard the small sound of something strange and intimate taking place and pounded the carpeted floor of their chamber with their angry hands.

She kissed his chin. She took one of his hands, which was curled into a half-hearted fist and flattened it out between her two hands. She kissed his hand.

He could not remember if she was tender. She was edited to sometimes be tender. But was she? She was murmuring something as she kissed him, but he couldn't understand what she was saying until he lowered his head to where her lips met his chest. "Is it you?" she was asking, "Is it you?"

What's more, he realized as his head came down to touch her head, she was not quietly kissing him, but smelling him. It was her nose, not her mouth, which left his skin damp and goosebumped where she touched him with it.

She smelled his forearm below the elbow crook. She

127

smelled his side just above his hip, where his jeans made a hard ridge beneath his t-shirt. He still smelled the same, which meant that this could not be happening. For a moment, she thought of the knife again. For a moment, she thought of another life entirely.

In the dark, the camera crew crept into a pile on the hard, hooked gray carpet. The places where they squeezed each other for reassurance were soft and sometimes moist.

For a moment, he looked at the knife stuck deep in the cutting block. For a moment, he could not imagine any part of the life that had come before this.

From the hall came a shrill noise, like the cry of an animal before it is eaten by a bigger animal. They both stood up straight. They both thought of the children, though each of them thought of a different child in particular.

The camera crew stood barefoot in the dark hallway. They were cold, they said. They couldn't sleep. Their hands were open and red, as if to show the source of their cold and sleeplessness.

She put apple slices in their hands. He marched them back downstairs. When he came back up, he said he thought he might watch reruns for just a little while before bed.

BETWEEN THE LAND AND THE SKY

That night, after their parents had called the very first family meeting ever, then given them the news, the brother and sister lay awake in single beds in their own dark rooms. Sister looked at the tiny stalactites dotting the ceiling and imagined that she was in an undiscovered cave, a mile underground. She shut her eyes very tight and heard the trickle of an underground stream, where eyeless fish darted and bumped into snot-slick rock. She smelled the mildew of a million years. She laid her sock monkey over her eyes. It was very dark.

Brother's ceiling was the night sky. Earlier that year, he had placed tiny glowing star stickers up there, arranged like real constellations. Because the ceiling was bumpy, sometimes stars fell onto him at night—Orion's belt buckle, the nose of Ursa Minor. As the galaxy shifted, he began to identify new constellations. Tonight, his eyes traced the lines of T-Rex and M-15. He counted down from ten and made a muted blasting sound with his small mouth. He would land on planet Heliotrope in eight Earth years and claim it for himself. He would terraform and tame the wild creatures that ran the plains. Sister could visit, but all other girls were banned forever, on pain of death.

Sister walked along the stream of the cave. Her flashlight made monstrous shadow puppets on the glittering walls. Under the bubbling of the water, Sister could make out a small scratching sound coming from a nearby vestibule. Sister turned her light toward it and the scratching became a moan, Doppling away from her, farther down the narrow passage. She took a step back, frightened, then followed the sound. After several yards, the corridor opened up. She was in Brother's room.

"Brother," she whispered and approached his bed. He lay silent and shivering. She put her flashlight on the floor and crept under his covers. His body was soft and hot. After a while, he turned toward her, still shaking. His nose moved against hers when he spoke. "The oxygen tanks," he gasped and was silent again. She put her hand on his chest and pressed her lips to his. She exhaled into him. He filled like a balloon and when he began to float away, he grasped her wrist and pulled her to him. They caught an updraft and began to rise uncertainly, their bodies pressed and bobbing, somewhere between the land and the sky.

BACTERIUM

{a member of a large group of unicellular microorganisms
(some of which cause disease)}

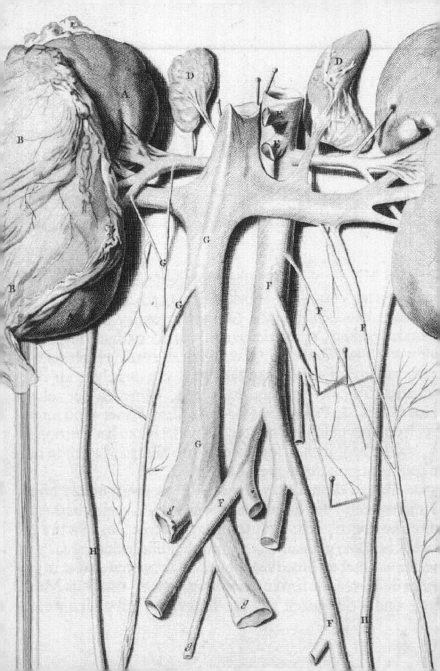

FIELD REPORTS

I.

Blood alcohol levels

   X: .07

   Y: .05

Setting

   Bar: Red-shadowed, hung with ghosts of smoked cigarettes

   No longer hazy but retaining a memory of haze

     Table: Tippy, salted, black

     Chairs: Ripped and tilted toward each other

Costuming

   X: Polyester wrap dress: black

     Heels: blister-raising, spine-arching

     Some Spanx™ shaping undergarments present

   Y: Jeans: designer

     Dress shirt: untucked, roll-sleeved, lavender

White ankle socks, brown driving loafers never worn
for driving

Upper bodies

X: Tabled at the elbow, hands turned in

Y: Right forearm tabled, left rests on thigh

Lower bodies

X: Foot pressed nervously into table leg

Y: Knee leaning outward, seeking

Pulse

X: 89 BPM

Y: 92 BPM

Notes

Some pupil dilation present (X and Y).

0134 EST

Blood alcohol levels

X: .16

Y: .11

Setting

Unchanged

Costuming

Unchanged

Upper bodies

X: Torso fully torsioned toward Y

Y: Right elbow closing distance, currently 5.3 inches from
left elbow of X

Lower bodies

X: A hopeful tingling

Y: Left knee: rhythmic

Pulse

X: 89 BPM

Y: 95 BPM

Notes

Phenylethylamine, dopamine, and norepinephrine levels
elevated (moderately: Y; slightly: X).

0215 EST

Blood alcohol levels

X: .19

Y: .13

Setting

Shared cab traveling uptown: smell of car deodorizer—cherry bark and almond. Leather seats: slightly shredded, impatient. Sodium street lamps blink by. Windows: lightly smeared (sebum/saliva) by previous passengers.

Costuming

X: Added: lightweight microfiber trench; six-dollar bodega umbrella—two broken spokes

Y: Added: gray lambswool pullover

Upper bodies

X: Head turned toward window

Y: Head turned toward head (X)

Lower bodies

X: Legs crossed toward Y

Y: Hoping for a fortuitous jostle

Pulse

X: 89 BPM

Y: 96 BPM

Notes

Slightly elevated blood pressure (Y).

0237 EST

Blood alcohol levels

X: .18

Y: .11

Setting

Front stoop: Brownstone, 1847, eight steps up to door

Weather: 55°F, breezy, 10% humidity, suggestive

Y stands on sidewalk, X one step above

Horizon lines:

> X: View of those deliciously cruel eyebrows, the slightly thinning crown, a 24-hour bodega across the street (Lucky Gem 24)

> Y: Eyes level with the swannish and pulsing neck of X—small, yellowed bruise the size of a thumbprint

Foliage: Boughs of city trees rustle above iron-fenced holes in the sidewalk. Not so much trees as reminders of trees. Trees like gravestones of trees.

Costuming   139

X: Lost: umbrella—back of cab. Bunched: Spanx™

Y: Lost: cellular telephone—back of cab; small percentage of nerve—back of cab

Upper bodies

    X: Lips, slightly parted

    Y: Hands, tensed to cup

Lower bodies

    X: Partly turned toward door

    Y: Partly erect

Pulse

    X: 90 BPM

    Y: 100 BPM

Notes

X makes false claims that situation is atypical. Y, gripping stair rail, practices the power of positive thinking™, wills bodies forward and up, toward entanglement.

II.

1434 EST

Blood alcohol level

X: .00

Setting

Waiting room on 33rd: Overlit and underpostered. Dirt in linoleum corners. One octagonal fish tank. One fish (Siamese fighting)

Seating: Wipeable, mauve, the smell of quick sanitation
Reading material: *Car and Driver* (1996), *TV Guide* (March 2001), *El SIDA y Tú* (hot pink and informational)

Costuming

X: Button-down shirt with permanent coffee stain, always claimed as new coffee stain when observed; black pants (polyester); cotton panties (breathable), as advised

Upper Body

Pulsing with beat of own heart

Lower Body

Symptomatic

Pulse

X: 96 BPM

Viral Load

Unknown

Notes

Siamese fighting fish (*Betta splendens*) are aggressive and tend to kill all but the most inconsequential of tankmates, such as shrimp. Betta are carnivorous and may eat their own fertilized eggs out of hunger.

1502 EST

Blood alcohol levels

X: .00

Y: .019

Setting

Exam room: Achingly cold, largely beige

Costuming

X: Paper gown, tied at neck, held at belly—one breast wandered out, nipple like a hex-giver, an evil eye, unnoticed by both

Y: Cotton overcoat, stained at neck and lapel. Stethoscope for show. Blue latex gloves.

Upper bodies

X: Reclined and chilly

Y: Hunched at shoulders, head straining forward as if preparing to enter, a breach birth in reverse

Lower bodies

X: Elevated and pushing out from inside, knees a million miles apart. A shuddering once the acid is applied. A pain sweat.

Y: Stool-perched

Pulse

X: 94 BPM

Y: 82 BPM

Viral Load

Est. moderate to high

Notes

Trichloroacetic acid, Interferon, Podophyllotoxin, Imiquimod, 5-Flourouracil (use discontinued due to burning), excision, diathermy, electrocauter, laser treatment.

1637 EST

Blood alcohol level

X: .18

Setting

Apartment bedroom

Bed: Queen-size HOPEN model from Elizabeth Center IKEA (1000 IKEA Drive, Elizabeth, NJ), chipped on delivery, slightly warped, modestly pillowed

Laptop: Warm on thighs

Internet: Borrowed from neighbors. CDC website strangely comforting; specialized dating sites, not

Cell phone: Opened and queued to call Y 40 minutes ago. No call made.

Costuming

None

Upper body

Irrelevant

Lower body

Scabbing, foreign

Pulse

X: 92 BPM

Notes

"Virus types are often referred to as 'low-risk' (wart-causing) or 'high-risk' (cancer-causing), based on whether they put a person at risk for cancer."

III.

1243 EST

Blood alcohol levels

    X: .12

    Y: .08

Setting

    Bar: Airplane-themed

        Table: Sunk with cupholders large enough for martini glasses

        Chairs: Fully padded yet still uncomfortable

Costuming

    X: Somewhat clever T-shirt, good ass jeans

    Y: White V-neck T-shirt, grey pants slightly tighter than they should be. The possibility of a hat or scarf.

Upper bodies

    X: Unnaturally upright and thrust forward toward Y, at shoulders. Tempted to palpate well-formed shoulders of Y.

    Y: Enticing clavicle view

Lower bodies

   X, Y: Knees pressed to knees, unacknowledged above the
        surface of the table between

Pulse

   X: 90 BPM

   Y: 90 BPM

Notes

   The American Airlines cocktail: Beefeater gin, dash of
   Mrs. T's Bloody Mary Mix (canned), peanut garnish.

0145 EST

Blood alcohol levels

   X: .15

   Y: .14

Setting

   The uptown 3: Smell of long-dried piss. Cornered away
   for the makeout. Pale selves reflected in windows that
   look onto nothing: subterranean ghosts. Surreptitiously
   photographed by lonely Goth. At the other end of the car,
   someone barely sings.

Costuming

    X: Added: faded blue hoodie

    Y: Added: black Members Only jacket

Upper bodies

    X, Y: Heads held by tongues in mouths of heads

Lower bodies

    X: Cross–legged and suddenly stung, as if to remind, as if in warning, as if moral compass of crotch outshone that of soul

    Y: One leg draped over crossed legs of X. Regretting tight pants.

Pulse

    X: 95 BPM

    Y: 90 BPM

Notes

    X screws up courage to notify. All is tight-wound, hard-pressed, horny.

0238 EST

Blood alcohol levels

    X: .14

    Y: .13

Setting

Bedroom: Moment of notification arrives.

Moment of notification passes, without notification. Y
lights candle. X extinguishes candle, wills Y not to see.

Costuming

X: None

Y: Black wool socks

Upper bodies

X: Arched to keep attention topside

Y: Attentive

Lower bodies

X: Leg wound over back (Y)

Y: Hip pressed to hip (X)

Pulse

X: 90 BPM

Y: 90 BPM

Notes

Copulations complete, X imagines a thousand vaginas,
identical to own, lined up forever, like mirrors on opposite
walls—an infinite regression. Like mirrors in grandparents'
bathroom, where X tried for hours to look through to the

end, but could never entirely get out of way of own self to see.

If X likes Y, then lies must be invented.

Y sleeps and dreams of airplanes.

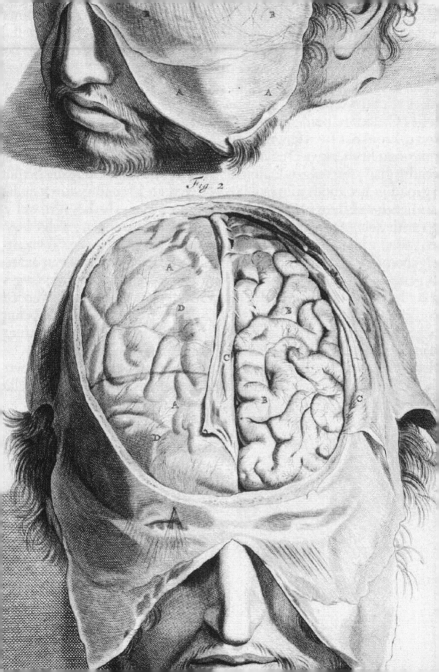

Fig. 2

ANOTHER ZOMBIE STORY

The zombie apocalypse took everyone by surprise, not because it was very different from all of the movies and books and television shows and songs about it, but because nearly everyone considered it not a real possibility but a metaphor about themselves. Back then, everyone thought everything was about themselves. People in failing relationships said things like, "It's not about you," by which they meant, "It's all about me." Children took guns to school and shot other children to see what it would feel like. People in positions of power did illegal things they did not even attempt to cover up and then were unapologetic when caught. Men put on Santa Claus suits and sprayed families with jet fuel, ignited it. No one saw it coming.

★

Out of habit and a long-standing sense of morbid curiosity, Dee logged onto EdenMatch and began to read through the profiles of the men who posted there. She was making a list of users who cited Dan Brown as their favorite or one of their favorite authors. The list was long and she wasn't sure what she would do with it once it was finished. Some days, she thought she might invite them to her house as a group and then set the house on fire. She wouldn't really do this, probably. But some days, it helped her to think she might. She didn't care why this was. She had stopped being very introspective some time ago.

No one on EdenMatch was very attractive, including herself, so it was different from online dating before in that the picture was no longer the main thing. In fact, many people didn't have pictures or even interests. Many people had interests that had nothing to do with the world they were currently living in. Ron, 47, liked parasailing and drive-in movies. He lived in Gated Community Orion, about three hundred miles from Dee's GC, Wonder, both of which were in what had been the state of Ohio. Ron had the usual scars and missing teeth, the usual weight put on from years of eating packaged, corn-based, junk food products, the usual ailments: scurvy. Dee had these things too, but she had recently stopped eating. Her last meal had been three days ago. She thought she might never eat again and see what happened to her. It was something to do.

An instant message popped up on her screen accompanied

by a picture of Jim. The photo had been taken at a distance—
he was mostly a shadow in a kitchen. The text of his message
said: "Lonely. You?"

"No," she wrote back.

"Want to meet? I'm the next GC over from yours—
Brookside."

"Do you like Dan Brown?" she asked.

"Who's Dan Brown?"

"You can come to my house at noon tomorrow," she
wrote and typed him the gate code then logged off. She
hadn't had a visitor in a very long time.

★

Before the zombie apocalypse, you could find anything
online, including the weather in any part of the world,
satellite photos of your local library, porn, paintings of famous
people with pancakes on their heads, Kurt Cobain's autopsy
photographs, mug shots of celebrities, recipes for Frito pie, and
videos of human decapitations. After the zombie apocalypse,
there was only internet dating.

155

★

When he came to the door, Jim looked like the shadow from his picture. He was dark, almost gray, even in the sun and close-up, Dee had trouble distinguishing his features. She had forgotten how to look at people—eyes first, down to mouth when it started talking, then away and back again, angling for a nose or cheekbone or eyebrow. She looked at his earlobe instead, which was actually the absence of an earlobe—soft ear tissue ending abruptly in tatters. So she focused on her mailbox, which lay behind him in the distance and rested, from her perspective, like a parrot on his shoulder.

"Can I come in?" he asked, both of them forgetting to introduce themselves.

She moved aside and waved her arm in front of her. He walked ahead of her like a butler into her kitchen.

"My house has the same floorplan," he said over his shoulder, beneath his ruined earlobe.

"Oh," she said. "In Brookside?"

"Yeah." He sat on a stool that stood beside a tiled island in the kitchen. She sat on the stool adjacent to his, not wanting to gaze or be gazed at.

They sat in silence for a minute, facing her bare white walls, until Jim asked, with some hesitation, "So. Do you want to have sex?"

She thought a moment and rubbed at a spot on a tile in

front of her, and unable to decide, said, "Okay."

*

Before the zombie apocalypse, some people liked to have a lot of sex. They talked about it all the time and made everyone who liked to have some sex or very little sex or no sex feel as though something was wrong with them. The people having a lot of sex felt bad for everyone else and wrote books about how to have better and better sex. There was no consensus on who was having the best sex though, which made it difficult to know which book to buy or which person to have sex with. Everywhere you looked, people were talking about the sex they were having or wished they were having, even children, which disturbed some people and excited others.

People especially liked to watch strangers have sex. The demand for this was so high that it was impossible to find enough strangers having sex at any given moment to meet it. As a result, VHS and digital video and the internet and web cams and virtual reality and sexy robots were invented. Pretty soon, people became lazy. Pretty soon, people stopped having sex with each other. Sex became a very private act. The feeling of someone's palm on your skin, or their hair in your mouth, or their toenails scraping your knee were universally understood to be distracting and intrusive.

★

Jim took Dee's hand and led her upstairs to her bedroom, to Dee's double bed. He held her hand at his chest and motioned for her to sit down. He placed her hand carefully in her lap and then took off his clothes. After he was naked, he took her hand again and beckoned her up. She stood and he took off her clothes as well, even her socks, which he crouched down low for. She put her hand on his head to steady herself.

Dee had never had sex with a real person before, but she didn't tell Jim this because she thought he might act weird or refuse to have sex with her entirely. She just wanted to know what it was like. It was like this: Everywhere he touched her felt very warm and then immediately cold after he withdrew his hand or his mouth or his leg. Her body became a checkerboard of cold and warm patches and he kept getting her wet with his spit and sweat and other stuff, and in the end, she felt shellacked, as if she could slip carefully out of the dried lacquer skin and it would keep its shape, her shape, like the husk of a cicada, fragile but whole.

"Are you hungry?" Jim asked, after they had been lying

there awhile.

"I'm not eating anymore," said Dee. "So, yes and no."

"Why aren't you eating anymore?" Jim asked.

"I don't like it," she said and shrugged.

"You don't like food?" he asked.

"I don't like any of it. I don't like anything anymore."

"Yeah," said Jim. He got up from the bed and put on his clothes. "I'll be right back," he said, and she listened to his carpeted footsteps move down the stairs and to the front door, which swooshed open then shut with a puffy, pneumatic sound.

She knew he wouldn't come back. She thought maybe she would wait the rest of it out here, in her shell on this bed, which she would slowly melt onto and dry into. Eventually, she would become the shell for this bed. The idea relaxed her.

★

Before the zombie apocalypse, when people were not used to thinking of themselves as food except in very extreme and disturbing circumstances often involving arctic weather conditions and poor planning, opinions about food were mixed. People loved and hated food. People who lived in Ethiopia and Beverly Hills did not eat enough food. People

159

who lived in Mississippi and Iowa, it was said, ate too much food. No one could find a balance. Some people didn't eat enough food because they had a disease. Other people ate too much food because they had another disease. Some people thought food could heal you or at least make you live longer. Others pointed out that certain foods might kill you, such as spinach, peanut butter, bread, anything prepared by frying, improperly processed and handled land meats, and many kinds of seafoods. It was a lot to consider. To make everything easier for everyone, eventually all food was made out of corn and processed crude oil and vitamin supplements. It was very cheap and had an incredibly long shelf life.

*

When Dee woke up, it was dark and there were sounds coming from her kitchen. She shivered into her pants and shirt, not bothering with the underwear. She grabbed her chef's knife and compact mirror from the drawer in her bedside table and heel-toed softly down the stairs and into the front hallway. She was not frightened but she was very alert. She tilted the mirror so that she could see around the corner and into the kitchen. Jim was there, his back hunched to her, his shoulders working. The island was strewn with plastic bags.

"Jim," she said, careful not to sneak up on him.

"There you are," said Jim and plucked the knife deftly from her hand as she approached him. "I was looking for that."

Everywhere there were vegetables. Cabbages and carrots lay like corpses in plastic-bag shrouds on the island. Kale leaves were stacked, waiting to be chopped on the counter near the sink. There were onions and tomatoes and celery stalks lolling on cutting boards. Something bubbled in a pot on a burner on top of the stove.

"What's going on?" Dee asked.

"I'm making lentil soup," said Jim.

"Where did you get all this...stuff?"

"From my garden," said Jim. "And it's not stuff, it's vegetables. Real food."

Dee's stomach rolled over itself. "I didn't know you gardened."

"Why should you?" he asked.

"You didn't list it as an interest in your profile," she said.

"I'm not really interested in it. I just do it so I don't have to eat Fritos all the time."

161

Dee didn't know how long it had been since she'd had real, live food. She worked a carrot out of an old Wal-Mart sack on the island. It was wet and dirty in spots and tiny hairs sprouted up and down the root. It tasted muddy and bright when she bit into it. Jim paused in his chopping and tossed her a kale stem and a wedge of onion, which filled her head with a stinging mist and made the small, hard walnut of her stomach expand and warm like a loaf of rising bread.

"It might make you sick at first," said Jim, "but you'll get used to it."

The lentil soup did make her sick. It was also very good. She asked Jim to show her how to make it, and the next night, he did.

★

Before the zombie apocalypse, people liked to measure their quality of life by considering whether or not they were happy. Some people were happy. Most people were varying degrees of unhappy. They bought things they thought might make them happy—expensive handbags, dogs, sexy robots, medications that increased the levels of serotonin in their brains—and sometimes they felt happier, but often they didn't. Some people suggested that this was what happened when everyone thought about themselves all the time. After the zombie apocalypse, people were tired of thinking at all.

They had seen and smelled and done things they wished they could scoop out of their brains and feed to the zombies. After the zombie apocalypse, people tried their best not to think about those things. Some people learned to make lentil soup. It was impossible to say if this made them happy or not.

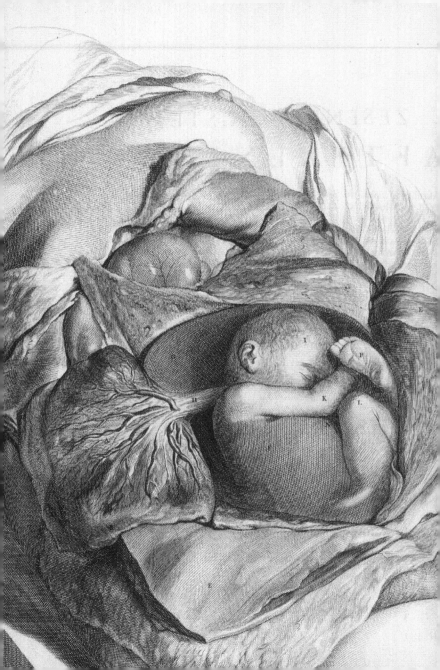

THE GOOD SON

When Jason passed her the roach, she took it gingerly from his thin fingers, as if this too were something she might kill.

"Okay, now suck in and hold it," Jason said, his puppy feet planted on the hard-packed dirt between them.

"I know how to smoke weed," she snipped. "Your generation didn't invent this." Jason looked down as his feet started to tap against each other, like Dorothy's ruby slippers.

"Whatever," he said.

"And anyway, you owe me."

"I didn't take no cigarettes," he spoke into the ground.

"You're a liar. I can tell—I used to be a teacher." She sucked on the soggy tip of the roach and coughed a little, recovered, took another hit. The smoke rolled out through the gaps in the makeshift smoking den Jason had constructed in his mom's backyard from three tarps, a few ropes, and a large patio umbrella he'd probably stolen from someone.

"Your mom doesn't come out here and check on you?"

"Nah," he said. "She works all the time. She doesn't

really care what I do, I'm just not supposed to get caught dealing again."

She looked at him through foggy eyes. "Dealing? Like drugs? Aren't you ten or something?"

"Twelve," he said fiercely as if this made all the difference in the world.

"Wow," she muttered, and because she was stoned, and hadn't yet gotten used to the idea of not thinking about it, she began to wonder what she would do, as a parent, twelve years in the future, if her baby started peddling dope. Everything a hypothetical. She closed her eyes and pushed the thought away.

There was something terribly ominous about how the doctor had called it her "first miscarriage" as if this were only the start. She hadn't realized what a broad term it was—miscarriage—how the thing that had happened to her mother, with blood and an ambulance and a hospital stay, could happen to her so quietly and unannounced. She had miscarried the baby. But it was still in her, just dead. She would go in for the D&C next week, the earliest her doctor could schedule it. Miscarry. As if she had been holding it wrong inside herself, as if this thing that had happened was her fault. Maybe it was.

She stood up, bent at the waist, a little woozy now from

all the wine she'd had earlier. "Thanks for the smoke. If I catch you on my porch again, I'm calling the cops." She threw open a tarp flap and lurched, squinting, into the sun, a cloud of smoke following her like an omen. Jason's two black lab puppies, sleek and fat as seals, lounged in the front yard beside the fence that separated her property from his. She leaned down to pet one and it lolled, sun sleepy, on its back. The other dog stood up and bowed before her, ready to play. "No," she said and opened the gate to the front yard. "I got nothing for you." Back in her living room, she finished the bottle of wine on the coffee table, closed the blinds, and put on *Aliens*.

★

Stephen had been crying so hard when they left the doctor's office that she decided to drive. His tears Rorschached out on the leather bucket seat wings. "Hey, at least we get to keep the Benz for a little while longer," she said just to say something. Their ancient Mercedes, which Stephen had bought for a thousand bucks in college, didn't have the seatbelt technology for the current baby seats, not even the cheap Wal-Mart ones that came in boxes covered in red Spanish. Stephen had told her he could hack the baby seat so it worked in the car, and she had said that hacking was okay for operating systems and coffee machines but probably not for safety devices intended to keep their future child alive. It was so hard, this idea of keeping a child alive. Next to impossible, she realized. Everything could go wrong. She put her hand to her lower belly. "Stephen?"

"I can't…" his voice was high and tight. "I can't talk right now, Mel."

"Okay."

She took a hard brake behind a car that suddenly decided to turn left and imagined the fetus inside her, popping through her belly button and smacking right through the windshield, up up into that dumb blue sky.

★

Though she had hoped the combination of pot and wine and the dark would convince her, finally, into sleep, she was all nerves as the mother alien spiraled into deep space. The movie had been a mistake. She felt the heaviness inside her now as a malevolent force that would rip her in two.

168

Her purse hung on the coat rack near the front door and she went to it, mindlessly gazing out the front west window as she picked out her phone. The woman who answered at the clinic sounded calm and motherly and told her she could get her in as early as tomorrow at 11. Mel was about to give her name to secure the appointment when her phone beeped—call waiting, Stephen. Her stomach turned and she took his call without another word to the receptionist.

"Hey," she said, afraid that he would know somehow about the call she'd just disconnected.

"What's going on over there? I've called like three times. I was getting worried."

"Oh," she said with forced nonchalance, "I must have had the ringer off." No word from him for a moment, then he spoke again, resentment hollowing out his voice.

"Well, if you're okay there, I have to stay late tonight. I was going to tell Joe I had to leave early, but he needs this shit done by tomorrow morning and I couldn't get a hold of you…"

As he talked and she responded with half-words, she watched out the window. A young hipster couple she'd never seen before walked up to the neighbor's fence and opened the gate. The guy had plugs and sleeves and the girl wore a vintage sundress. The lab puppies wagged hard at them and jumped, nipping at the leash the man held. The girl leaned down to pet both the dogs but stood up again when one of them clawed at her shoulders in excitement. They both walked to the door of the neighbor's house and after a moment, Jason opened it and let them in. As they walked inside, the guy took his wallet out of his back pocket.

"Mel?"

"Yeah, I'm—I'm fine here, Stephen. It's okay."

"Fine," he said but didn't hang up.

"Okay," she said.

"Do you want me to bring you anything?"

"Cigarettes," she said.

"Not a chance. I love you." He hung up before she could say it back.

As Mel stood at the window with the phone still at her ear, the couple came out of the house. The girl pointed at the smaller dog, the one Jason called Snaps, and the man hoisted it up as the girl attached the dangling leash to its collar. The couple shut the front gate behind them and put Snaps on the sidewalk. The other puppy—Mel couldn't remember the name—barked and raced back and forth along the fence as the strangers walked off toward the corner, toward the busy thoroughfare that ran perpendicular to their street. Snaps stiffened his legs until his leash was taut, and looked back at the other dog who was barking and bouncing at the fence between them. But Snaps was clearly excited to be out beyond the confines of his yard and when the guy yanked hard on the leash, Snaps acquiesced, deciding in a quick, dog second to leave it all behind.

*

Once home from the doctor, they had lay down on their bed, the Tempurpedic king-size they'd bought for themselves with their savings. One last gift before the baby came and vanished the money from their accounts like a magician or a con. They talked about a trip to Mexico, but in the end, their shared practicality won out. This was something they'd always appreciated about each other, these easy agreements about how to spend money. It was, she knew, because they'd both come from similar families. His mother a casino bunny, her father the best dressed man on layaway. These small things, they'd always thought, would shelter them from their human share of heartaches. Now, as she curled her knees to her chest, his hand heavy on her hip, she felt the bed was less a shared vision than a cushy sinking monument to the baby. When he started to snore, she got up and moved to the couch in the living room.

*

She watched as Jason came out of the front door a few seconds later, looked furtively around, then walked out of the front gate, and, whistling, went the opposite way the couple had gone. The remaining puppy jumped up on the fence and whined as it watched him go.

Mel's hand shook slightly as she dialed the clinic again. The appointment was still available, the woman said. Did she have a ride home, or would she need the free taxi service the clinic could provide? If she chose the taxi service, they'd have to keep her a little longer, to make sure she was not hemorrhaging.

"How much longer?"

"A couple of hours. You'd be home by three."

"Okay," she said and moved away from the window, back to the dark interior of the living room.

The second bottle of wine began to calm her almost immediately and she watched *The Good Son* with something like light in her belly. She drunkenly cheered Macauley Culkin's fatal cliff fall. The thing inside her was a Culkin. The thing inside her was a Jason in the making.

172 After the movie, she went to the front porch to smoke a cigarette. Jason's mother was home from work, pacing her own stoop, with her phone at her ear and a cigarette jutting between her French-manicured nails like an exclamation

point. She sounded angry. Mel tried not to listen, but the woman had a tendency to perform for the neighborhood.

"And I'm telling you, I want an officer over here now. What if I told you my house got broken into?"

There was a pause as she listened, smoking quickly, like upset people do in movies.

"No, I'm not saying that. I'm saying, a dog is property, just like a flatscreen TV. I want somebody over here so I can file a report. Yeah? Okay." Smoke smoke smoke. "Fine."

The neighbor hung up and swore. Mel tried to light her cigarette quietly—maybe she would escape detection and be spared the small talk—but the neighbor's head turned at the flick of Mel's lighter.

"Hey," she said, stepping close to the fence between their yards. They'd lived next door to each other for two years, but the neighbor had never bothered to learn her name. The neighbor's name was Nancy, but Mel refused to use it.

"Hey," Mel said and half-waved but didn't make eye contact.

"Some asshole stole my dog." Nancy said this accusingly, as if she believed that asshole might be Mel.

"Oh." Mel made what she hoped was a surprised and sorry face. "Oh no, that's awful."

Nancy nodded, "Yeah, some asshole just came into my

yard while I was at work and took her. Can you believe that?"

Mel felt caught. She cleared her throat. "Did Jason see anything?"

Nancy shook her head, "He was at the skatepark all day." She shook her head again and looked vaguely around the neighborhood. When she turned back, she was crying. "What kind of stinkin' asshole would do something like that? And the cops. They can't even come over till tomorrow they're so busy. Tomorrow! If there was a trail or a lead, it'll be gone by tomorrow, that's for sure."

Mel wasn't sure what kind of trail she meant or what the means of detecting such a thing might be.

"If I told that kid once, I told him a million times to put the dogs in when he goes out. But he's...he's off his meds right now and out of school. No structure. You should see him in there, bawling his eyes out. This might finally send him over the edge. He has psychological problems, you know." Nancy had said this same exact thing to Mel maybe fifty times.

"Wow," said Mel, feeling more and more like a mechanical doll whose cord had been pulled. "I'm sorry."

"So you didn't see anything?" Nancy asked quietly, the fight gone out of her.

Mel shook her head and put out her cigarette. "I'm sorry, Nancy."

Nancy was looking up at the sky, muttering, "Who would do that? What asshole?" as Mel walked back into the house and shut the door.

★

That night, he had woken her on the couch and asked her what she wanted from the grocery store. Wine, she said, and cigarettes. And stop at Blockbuster too—*Rosemary's Baby*, *Aliens*, and *The Omen*, maybe *We Need to Talk about Kevin* or *The Good Son* if they didn't have the others. He came back with vanilla ice cream, root beer, and *Buffy the Vampire Slayer*. She sat as far away from him on the couch as she could and glared as he spooned down his float.

"You could have at least rented the TV series," she said finally. "The movie is a terrible piece of shit." He scooted over to her and kissed the side of her head and tried to feed her a spoonful of ice cream but she crossed her arms, like a child, and squeezed her eyes shut.

"Our first date," he said. "Remember?" She did. She knew. Slightly drunk and back from the college bar where they'd been eyeing each other for weeks. Her roommate had fired up the movie and smoked them out and instead of moving into her bedroom, they'd passed out together on the floor in front of the TV, more embarrassed in the morning than they would've been if they'd actually hooked up.

She sighed and put a hand on his leg. "This isn't about us," she said. "This is about me."

He removed her hand and got up, walked into the kitchen, threw his glass into the sink where it shattered, and went to bed.

★

When Stephen finally came home, she had fallen asleep in bed with the movie going. Had moved the TV from the living room where it usually lived because TV in bed is supposed to be bad for the sex life of a couple. The sudden quiet when he turned it off is what woke her, though she pretended to be asleep until he crawled under the covers and palmed her shoulder, turning her to him gently, his face slightly green in the light of the alarm clock. He apologized first. He didn't even say for what. This was always his way. Apologizing when things were going wrong, even if it wasn't his fault. This loosened something inside Mel and she began, finally, to cry loudly next to him. He looked relieved and wrapped himself around her under the covers.

"What happened today?" he asked when she had caught

her breath. And that was the moment she should have told him about scheduling a new abortion for tomorrow, without him, but he might have been angry, even in this dark and softened room, and she didn't know if she could bear another day with the thing inside her, but she also didn't know if she could bear to go there without him, to sit next to those fertile, stoic teens and their mothers, their boyfriends, all getting a choice in the matter when she'd been given none. She didn't think she could say anything at all to him because she was just so tired.

"Somebody stole one of the neighbor's puppies," she said after a while.

"Oh, man," he said. "What happened?"

And now she just wanted to go to sleep and not explain anything else because one explanation led to another and there would be so much explaining to do in the coming days to their families and friends. She just couldn't.

"I don't know," she said. "Nancy was upset though." Then she kissed his neck and rolled away from him, and when he touched her again, it was after she was already asleep and had no sense of his arm there like a tether, keeping her tied to the earth as firmly as he could.

★

After the doctor's appointment, she had thought about going to work the next day, then thought about all the maternity leave she wouldn't be taking, and called in. She was the office manager for a small educational textbook publisher. In college, she'd wanted to be a teacher, but had terrible stage fright in front of the classroom as a student teacher. Then this job came along and it made her feel connected to teaching without actually having to teach. Mostly, she ordered pens and Wite-Out and took care of scheduling and scanned things now when she used to fax them. The thing she liked most about her job was that it required nothing of her that any other person in the office couldn't do themselves. She decided not to go in for the rest of the week. Stephen also wanted to call in sick but she couldn't have this. She wanted to be alone in the dark. "You have to be the rock right now," she said to him.

"Fine," he said, "But I want you to know this is about me too whether or not you want it to be."

"I know," she said but didn't really feel this way. She watched him pull out of the driveway and turn onto the main road and then she went to the grocery store and Blockbuster. When she got home, she dropped her packages inside, then sat on her porch and lit her first cigarette in three years. She'd bought two packs at the store. It felt like a commitment.

The initial drag edged her vision with a kind of dark static and she thought she might pass out. It was disgusting and delicious. Like a fly to shit, she thought as she filled the invisible creases of her lungs, the cigarette reminding her that they were there, just above the baby, two toxic balloons. She finished and stubbed out the butt on the bottom of her shoe, leaving the pack on the arm of the Adirondack chair.

Inside, she opened the first bottle of wine, put on *The Omen*. She liked the vampiric way the priest said, "The child is dead. He breathed for a moment. Then he breathed no more," with a slight roll of the *r*. "Drink up," she trilled to her uterus and raised a toast to nothing.

She was three glasses of Pinot in when she saw a flash of movement in the front window that overlooked her porch. When she opened the door, she saw Jason. Even though it was nearly ninety degrees, he was wearing an oversized button-down shirt, like a kid playing dress up. She had only a second to process the startled look on his face, the flash of white in his hand and the way that hand retracted up into the sleeve of the shirt before he was blurting out something about her yard.

"What?" she asked, fuzzy.

"Do you need it mowed?" he asked. Then, oddly, "I thought you guys were at work."

Even through the wine, she could sense that something

179

was off. And then—she saw it without seeing it—something in her brain connected: the pack of cigarettes was gone from the chair. Jason was leaning away from her, his small body pointed toward the porch stairs, ready to run.

She squinted at him. "If you thought we were gone, why would you come over to ask us about our lawn?"

He shrugged, still wide-eyed, and she caught the furtive movement of the hand up his sleeve.

"Give me back my cigarettes," she said.

He looked at her with a confusion that was almost convincing. "I don't know what you're talking about."

"Give me back my cigarettes or I'll tell Nancy you smoke weed in that tent you have in your backyard."

His mouth opened and closed and opened again. She was watching his delinquenty little brain work.

"Yeah, I know all about that. I can smell it when I'm in bed at night," she said. Then: an idea. "Or you can smoke me out and I'll let you keep the cigarettes. Fair trade."

Now it was his turn to squint. He looked left and right in a way that was too sophisticated for his age. Then he seemed to decide something. "Okay," he whispered. "You can smoke some, but it's because I like you. You and Stephen. I didn't take your cigarettes."

"Sure," she said. "Let's get to it." And as she followed him across her lawn to the sidewalk and through the metal gate, where his dogs waited to greet them like the most loving of children, she thought that this is how it begins, the letting go. And she allowed the idea of the baby, which she had kept so close these months, to start to slip away from her like a half-remembered movie, like something she had once dreamed.

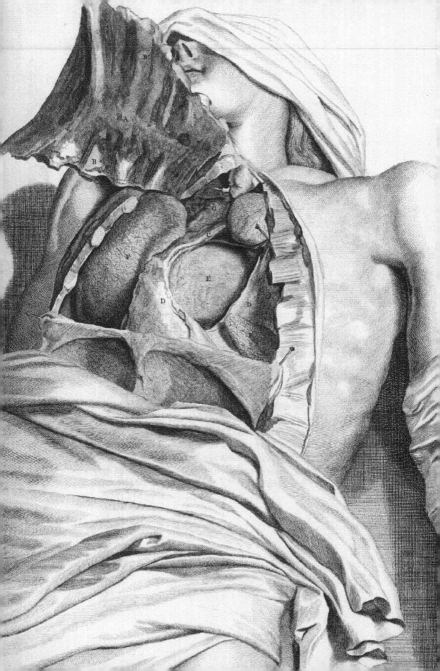

SHEARING DAY

Fifteen pills in the morning. He could feel them press through the skinny path of his trachea, like a finger, tracing him from the inside. Every morning he told himself a story while he took them, one at a time, dropped from his fist into his tilted head like a baby bird. The regurgitant of science. Dead without.

The story went: Once upon a time, there was a prince born with a broken heart. He was a good prince and did many things right in his life—got good grades, did not swear that much, had never smoked weed, even when Jason passed him a joint behind Koser's Ice Cream in eighth grade and then made fun of him and, eventually, stopped being his friend. But the prince was always sad. His heart sat useless and bricky in his chest. There was nothing anyone could do to fix it until one day, a beautiful princess traveled with her coterie to the prince's kingdom. She fell in love with the prince at first sight. For his part, for the first time, the prince felt some sleepy light blink on inside him, then shudder out.

The princess said to the prince, "You cannot love me

with a broken heart. If you take my heart then we shall always be together and your heart will be full of my love." The prince said, "But what will become of you?" and the princess said, "I will live in you." And the prince thought about it and thought about it and finally agreed—for their love was not true as long as his heart was broken. The princess kissed him once, then turned into a dove and pierced his chest with her beak. The prince fell to the ground, fast asleep. When he awoke, he felt the dove fluttering inside his chest and all the love in the world rushed on him at once. And he cried and gnashed his teeth because the princess, his true love, was deep inside him now and he would never see her again.

Randy sucked the last pill from his fist where it had already begun to dissolve in his sweaty palm, then wiped his hand on his jeans, went to the fridge, and drank from the carton of O.J. Sometimes he liked to think of the princess as Melinda Rhead, from art class. She liked video games too and they swapped sometimes. She knew about him, but she didn't care because she was new this year and had her own crap to figure out. He thought he might love her but he wasn't sure how you told someone something like that, or even figured it, for sure, for yourself. He could tell her his story, maybe, and if she liked it, great. If she thought it was stupid and babyish, well, then he'd know something.

The busy sound of his mother preceded her into the kitchen. "Take all your pills?" she was bustling at the purse on her hip, rummaging around fruitlessly. She looked up at him with a sigh. "Linda called. They're shearing today and she needs help with the food. Thought you and Will might like to see each other. Play some video games maybe. So go get ready." She swept out again, still busy in her purse, still looking, it seemed, for some imagined thing that lay hidden, just out of view.

Randy gathered some video games from his stack in the living room and stuffed a couple in the front pocket of his sweatshirt. He hadn't seen Will in three months, but he knew, from overheard phone conversations, that Will's heart "took." That's how his mom put it on the phone to his aunt. "Will's heart took. And you know, I'm glad for them. I'm happy for Linda. But it's hard for me to talk to her lately. It's always 'Will's grown six inches,' or 'Will helped his dad with all the chores this morning.' When will that be us?"

Randy thumbed the side of a game cartridge in his pocket and thought of the hospital bed, his home for six months. All he knew is he didn't want to go back. He'd rather be dead.

★

Will loped up the steep west hill of the pasture of his family's farm. His approach scattered the crias, whose mothers bleated warnings as he passed by. The new barn at the top of the hill housed the alpacas, but the animals were scattered all over the pasture today because of the work going on in the barn. Will could hear the shouts of the men from inside and every now and then, an alpaca would come careening, panicked, out of the huge open doors, nearly ramming the fence before veering off into the field. Will's destination was the old barn, just a few hundred feet away, lower on the slope. It was ancient and dark and housed all the animals they'd raised before his parents had caught alpaca fever. There were hens and geese and a goat or two, but mostly sheep, cowering in the corners. They'd run into the barn when the alpaca had first appeared and had settled in ever since, stupidly afraid of the interlopers. They were old and tough and good for nothing in their smelly, overgrown wool that no one bothered to shear anymore. It wouldn't bring even a fifth of what an alpaca fleece could get. And so he was put in charge of them, the forgotten rotting sheep. It was like they didn't trust him with their babies, those strange Huacayas with their giant eyes and bird warbles.

Will disliked the alpaca for their pretensions—that fancy crimp, their pricey wool—but he hated the sheep. "You stupid…pussies," he said to them as they bleated from their corners while he filled their water troughs with the hose. He liked how the word felt in his mouth. Being a serious Bible student, he was not used to swearing. It didn't come naturally. When he did manage to push something dirty out of his mouth, it always burst out crazy-sounding, loud and out of control—like a flock of flushed partridge. Will thought it was a good idea to practice because today was shearing day, and Craig would come again, like he did every year. Will wanted to impress him.

It was the first shearing day since his surgery and he felt strong. He had grown six inches in the last few months. He had been lifting weights. Once a picky and delicate eater, he now ate constantly. He ate everything. He might never stop growing. He wanted to crush things in his newly bigger hands.

Craig could lift an adult alpaca in his arms and carry it, kicking and spitting, across the barn without a faltering step. When his parents weren't watching, Will practiced catching the yearlings in the far field and hoisting them up as far as he could. It made his new heart pound furiously, forced the blood through him so hard he could almost feel it pushing him out, making him larger, his flesh giving in to the awesome power of the tides that now pulsed inside him.

He finished filling the water troughs and wound the hose

onto its wheel. Men from neighboring farms, and from farms as far away as Michigan, were already at work in the new barn, laying out the wooden shearing platforms and hoist systems that would keep the alpaca stretched and prone while Craig's clippers worked through the fleece. Breeders and farmers were arriving every minute and they chased their animals out into the field. They would have about four hundred animals to get through once Craig arrived. Will was ready.

★

"Can I drive?" Randy asked, but his mom was already sinking herself into the beige leather driver's seat. She opened the garage door and rolled down the passenger-side window.

"Get in, Randy, we're running late."

"I want to drive," he said but he knew how his mom was.

"Randy, get in. We're late and it's too…I just don't think it's a good idea for you to be driving yet. We've already talked about this."

Randy stood silently near the car. His old Flexible Flyer hung on the garage wall, spiderwebbed and rusted, put up for good after the doctor had diagnosed catastrophic heart failure. He remembered the last weekend he had taken it out to a golf course a mile away from the house. The snow was two feet deep and higher where it had drifted. They'd all been stuck inside for three days during the storm and this felt like a hard-won freedom. The sun cut through the sky like glass as he waded through the snow. His heartbeat filled his whole body, warmed him inside out, fell into his groin on that first wild hill. The copper taste in the back of his throat, his lungs pinching through his side, the brilliance of the sky as his sled banked itself and he flew forward into the soft lap of the new snow. The warm, wooly smell of spit and sweat and ice on his facemask. He thought of that last day of sledding as the last day of his life.

His mother backed the car out of the garage. In the old days, she would have honked, started the garage door down so he'd have to run and duck to get under it, but now, even after the transplant, she was so afraid.

"Get your butt in here now," she yelled. He kicked at a case of Diet Coke on the floor, hoping she'd get sprayed next time she opened one, and walked through the garage to the driveway.

*

Will and his father had just finished herding the last of the reluctant alpaca from the field into the holding pen when he got a text from his mom. Randy and Pam were at the house. Come down and say hello.

"Oh...shit," said Will. His father, who was tethering the gate to the holding pen closed, gave him a sharp look.

"What's wrong, man?"

"Nothing. I'm okay. I just have to get back down to the house."

His father relaxed, "Take it easy today, okay? I know you want to help Craig and his team, and that's great, but they're professionals. Try not to get in their way. And don't...don't overexert yourself. I've gotta go into town for a while. You help your mom run food and drinks up, okay?"

Will shot his father a nasty look and shook his head, then set out for the house at a sprint. He could feel his dad's eyes on him all the way down the hill and he sped up, exaggerating the motion of his arms and legs, whipping across the pasture grass and leaping the divots and rabbit holes. He burst into the front hallway where his mom stood with Pam and Randy.

"Will, you've gotten even bigger...again, I swear." Pam gave him a long, wincing look, then enveloped him in a hug that smelled like perfume and boiled potatoes. The smell hung around even after she'd moved into the kitchen with his mom.

"What's up, Will?" Randy smiled but Will could see he

was exhausted. His eyes were big in his head and rimmed in shadows. His skinny frame sunk into itself at the shoulders. Will looked away. He recognized that body. It had been his not long ago. He swallowed to settle the disgust that blossomed in his stomach. "Hey man, how's it going?"

"I'm cool. What about you? You're taller."

"Yeah. I'm good. Just helping with the shearing. Didn't know you guys would be here today."

"Yeah, your mom called my mom. Your mom says she gets bored cooking down here by herself all day. So we came over."

Will was only half listening to Randy. He was trying to catch the low conversation coming from the kitchen. Doctors weren't happy. Minimal progress. Possible rejection.

Will put a hand on Randy's shoulder. "You want to go see the shearing? They're going to start any minute."

"No, Randy," yelled Pam from the kitchen. And in a sniff, she was at Randy's side, taking his coat off of him like he was five. "How about you guys play some video games downstairs?"

"But they're about to start up the hill."

"Will!" Pam barked. Adults were rarely sharp with him and it made him feel hot and hateful to hear her yell. Without a word, he turned and walked down the basement stairs and Randy followed without comment or apology.

★

Video games had brought them together in the first place. Their mothers had both walked into the PICU carrying new Xbox 360 systems on the same day. Both had sons almost the same age waiting for heart transplants. Both congenital defects from birth. Will and Randy had been separated on the ward, each imprisoned in his own private pediatric intensive care room, immobilized by the monitors and machines that kept their tired hearts beating. But they could talk to each other on their own Xbox Live network. And as they drove over cops and pushed back Covenant alien attacks and did the only boyish thing left to them in the world, they talked.

Sometimes about how much they hated the wallpaper— giant stick children drawn by artsy adults, made to look infantile, in bright, basic colors, with a whiff of the crayon about them. Sometimes they talked about dying and said brave, untrue things like, "I've lived a good, full life" and "It's all in Christ's hands now." Will wanted to be a minister. Randy wanted to design video games. Both could appreciate where the other was coming from.

★

That had been a long time ago. Six inches of growth ago. It had been in the weak time, but the weak time was over. When Randy asked if he had any new games, Will, without even thinking about it, almost didn't answer him. As if Randy had never spoken. As if he weren't there. Will thought of Jesus in Capernaum and Gennesaret and all the people he healed. And for the first time, he thought how hard that must have been. And how, if he were Jesus, he'd have totally hated sick people by the end.

"I don't really play video games anymore. I've been really into working out and stuff."

"Oh. Yeah, that's cool. Do you, like, have a girlfriend or something?"

"Yeah. I have a couple."

"Do you play video games with them? Because there's this one girl in my—"

"You don't play video games with girls, dummy," Will squinted at Randy. "You drive them out to some field and get them to take off their shirts."

Randy's mouth opened in surprise and Will felt that disgust rising in him again. He wanted to push it up against Randy, to rub his nose in it like a bad dog. "Then, you know, sometimes you get to touch their...their titties." Will tried to smirk, but he already felt bad about saying it, wished he could

193

take it back.

Randy closed his mouth and cleared his throat. "I don't know about that. But...I brought The Darkness with me. I can show you how to play." Randy took a game out of his hoodie pouch and loaded it.

"I guess," said Will and sat on the couch while Randy folded himself into a slump on the floor.

"So the main thing is, you're Jackie, and you're possessed by The Darkness, which is this spirit thing which is evil but also helps you. It's like the new Grand Theft Auto, where you can do missions or just run around New York and shoot people." Randy demoed a short mission and Will thought a little more about Jesus and picked up the controller and they started a new game. For a while, the only sound was the hard industrial grind of the game music, turned low, and the soft click of the controllers in their hands.

"Hey Will," said Randy.

"Yeah," Will said, distracted as he tried to put a bullet in the face of a mob guy.

"Did your dick get bigger too?"

Will was silent a minute. "That's a weird question."

"Well, the rest of you got bigger. I just wonder. If they get my transplant working right, I just want to know if my dick's gonna get bigger too."

"Yeah, I guess. I mean, I don't know. I don't think we should talk about it though." Will put his controller down. "Let's get out of here. They're shearing up the hill. The shearing guy is from New Zealand. He's, like, crazy strong. I'm supposed to be helping him this year. He's gonna be mad if I stay down here all day."

"I don't think I'm supposed to leave. I might get in trouble."

"Come on, don't be a…a pussy."

Randy squinted at Will. "I'm not a pussy."

Will looked at the ground, "I didn't mean…let's just stay here. This game is kind of cool."

Randy put his controller down, walked to the sliding glass doors and pulled at them, breathing hard. Will followed him out of the house and took the lead. They cut around the side of the hill that rose above them, skirted it through the steep west pasture where they couldn't be easily seen from the house. It was a cool April, but Randy was sweating. His breath came shallow and fast. Will stopped and pretended to count some of the sheep that had fled the noise and gathering crowd on the hilltop.

195

"Let's just rest here for a minute," he said, but Randy pretended not to hear him and so they both kept walking.

★

There were almost as many people in the barn as animals, whose screams seemed distant from outside the barn, but piercing and nearly unbearable inside. Utterly ignoring the noise, a few tight-haired older ladies in sweatshirts sat at a long table set up on the side of the barn, talking and labeling fleece bags and making official note of each animal being sheared. A few couples stood around silently, faces deep in coffee cups. Little kids kicked around in the piles of castoff wool accumulating in the corners of the barn.

There were three shearing stations, with two men on each pulley, two men to mind and rope each animal, and two fleecers crouched at the side of each platform to gather the wool as it was shorn and arm-sweep it into clear bags that were named and numbered. Each animal was led, whimpering from the holding pen. When the animal arrived at a shearing station, a sock was quickly stuffed over its snout to intercept the stinking green bile it would begin to spit when its front and hind legs were roped and stretched tight away from its body. Laying the alpaca out in midair, the pulley workers then gently lowered it onto the platform, where Craig would kneel on it, clippers already chewing air, and work the fleece free of the skin in long, wide strips. Back and sides first, then legs, and finally, neck and topknot. Then onto the next station where a new animal was laid out and waiting. Craig worked the room like a dervish.

"They have to work really fast," Will yelled to Randy above the noise. "He has to shear like four hundred in one day. People bring in their animals from everywhere—he's that good. He flies all the way from New Zealand to shear all over the country every spring." Craig, with his long blond hair, black coveralls and rubber kneepads looked like some kind of superhero.

"It smells disgusting," Randy huffed from beneath the cuff of his sweatshirt.

"It's the spit. It's really gross. Don't get any on you."

The boys watched from the side of the barn for a while. When Craig called a break, Will pulled Randy's shirt, "Come on, I gotta see if he needs me." But Randy hung back. He thought Will, whom he had once considered his best friend, was acting like a big asshole. Randy smiled. Big asshole for the big new body. Maybe if his heart had worked as well as Will's, he would be a big asshole now too.

Randy watched Will talk to Craig. Watched Craig's squint deepen. Watched Craig look around, like he was looking for help, come up blank, then begin to nod. Will walked back to the holding pens and Craig called one of the pulley men over and pointed at Will. The man nodded and Craig called the break with a whistle he fished from a breast pocket.

Their momentum broken, the men started off slower than they'd finished. Will led an alpaca to the first station, helped loop its back feet, and then walked around to the front of the platform to take the rope that would pull the front legs straight. He nodded as one of the shearing team pointed and shouted instructions. "Front legs is weaker than the back, but they'll still kick, so hold tight."

Will squatted beside the platform, pulling the rope tight to hold the animal in place. There was a subtle back-and-forth between Will and the other rope guy as they lowered the splayed animal down to the platform. The professional rope man was trying to find a balance, letting out and pulling in slightly as Will struggled, sweated, and grimaced with his end. The alpaca landed gently and Craig pounced. Will and the rope guy fell to their knees in unison. Craig finished shearing and Will freed the beast, walked it to the finishing pen, secured the gate, and wrangled another mewling animal to be shorn. The whole room worked like a machine and Randy felt lulled as the team became more fluid and faster as they worked the break out of themselves.

Craig was amazing to watch. His movements were so

spare and quick. Not a turn or a reach wasted. He buzzed through animal after animal. Randy imagined Craig's heart made a sound as regular as the ticking of a metronome. But stronger, thuddier. A slowed-down jackhammer. A pile driver.

Randy was invisible in this corner of the barn and he liked it that way. Liked to watch people who didn't watch him back. No nurses or doctors or parents or teachers waiting for a sign, a twitch. Waiting for him to start to die. He relaxed and blew a clump of floating gray wool away from his mouth and watched it ascend, so light it might never come down.

Randy was lost in the rafters when he heard the first scream, felt his heart jump awkwardly then begin to race before he could make sense of the scene in front of him. There was Will, painted in blood, and standing, mouth open, rope at his feet. The alpaca was pawing at the platform with its front feet and Craig yelled, "Hold it!" as two men from the other stations leapt across their platforms and landed on the struggling animal, whose neck was spitting blood. It was the animal that was screaming. And as Randy understood this, the screaming stopped. There was a beat of silence, then frantic human voices began to echo through the barn, piling up and catching on each other like strands of loose wool. Two men took off for the house. Craig was working at the animal's neck with a tube of superglue. His hands and the tube were slick with blood.

"Won't fucking stick!" he yelled, as his hands scrambled in the mess. But the alpaca was already limp. It had stopped kicking and its eyes had quit rolling in panic. They stared ahead at nothing; they stared at Randy.

Craig looked at his hands and then up at Will. "What the fuck you doing standing there? What the fuck is wrong with you? You didn't see the fucking clippers was already going?"

Will's jaw began to shiver, "I didn't...the rope slipped out—"

"Get out of here! Go tell your dad you just cost him fifty thousand dollars!"

Will was crying now, but didn't move. Two men unroped the dead alpaca and dragged it into the dirt at the mouth of the barn. They were followed by a small, wide-eyed crowd. Randy put a hand on Will's arm and pulled at him. He came without resistance. Randy walked them past the dead animal, through the crush of people who swarmed it like flies. The boys tripped down to the old barn and tucked away just as a group ran by from the house, Pam and Will's mom among them. Randy froze at the sight of them—rushing and stone-faced, saving it all up for the panic and the anger that would soon follow. He plucked at Will's shirt and backed him up to the corner of the barn, next to the sheep pen where a dove cooed on a post and an old buck eyed them suspiciously, its head half-buried in a feedbag. The boys sat hard in the dirt, shoulders touching, legs crossed, shivering, the stink of blood thick between them, hearts working furiously toward each other in the sun-spiked shadows.

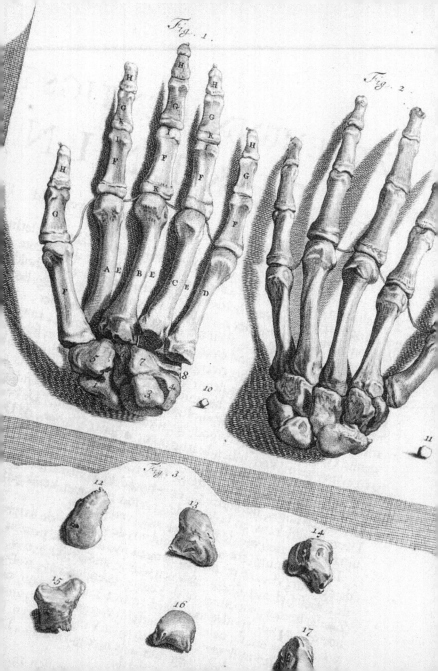

LIKE ACROBATS

Keohane was working up a fiberglass rash that would bother him for weeks. He could feel grit in the folds of his neck every time he raised his head. His crew had been on the job for only eleven days now, but they were already beginning to complain. It wasn't just the sticky heat of late summer in Boston—a particularly bad one this year—or the brutal work of an enormous teardown project. It was the job itself, the finals stages of the Boston Garden demolition, that had his men sore. Most were from old Italian and Irish families in the neighborhood and had spent their young summers playing pick-up ball in the parking lot. That few of them could afford to get through the front gates was beside the point.

Keohane wiped his neck with a handkerchief and surveyed the mess. The wrecking crews had been here first, leveling the structure with dynamite and bulldozers. He was here to take the rest apart and haul it off. He'd like to keep a piece—maybe a bit of the foundation—or a chunk of Tony-O's, the pizza joint that had stood just north of the Garden where the Fleet Center now rose, clean and new like a fancy stranger just come to town.

His son would have liked a brick from the restaurant. Michael, at five, sitting glass-eyed in the green vinyl booths, hypnotized by the tapes of boxing matches that looped on the televisions in each corner of the restaurant, legs not yet long enough to reach the ground.

"Hey, Boss, need some help!" McConnell yelled from across the vast expanse of asphalt. He began to jog toward Keohane, left wrist held against his body with his right hand.

Keohane cursed under his breath as he watched McConnell approach and stuffed his rag into the back pocket of his work pants. "What am I, a medic?"

McConnell caught up to him, wincing, in front of the bed. "Bids dropped a wicked heavy sledge on my hand. I think he broke the middle one."

Keohane reached inside the truck for the kit. "All right, let's see it." McConnell smiled and flipped him a sad little bird, his middle finger bent all wrong and swelling. Keohane flicked the finger hard and McConnell's laugh caught in his throat and he pulled his hand back into his stomach protectively.

"Looks like a sprain, Mary."

McConnell held out his hand again and squeezed his eyes shut as Keohane shimmied a foam and metal splint over the finger. The top knuckle looked ready to burst out of the skin.

It was probably broken, but no one needed to hear that right now. Already the crew was working with a major concussion that had put Grenham out a few days, and an assortment of cuts and bruises that had everyone skittish.

"Bad luck, man. This job is just bad fucking luck," said McConnell as Keohane finished with tape to keep the splint in place. It would be bad for sure when the contractor got wind of all the comp claims for the month. Keohane knew his guys would keep quiet about the pussy stuff, but even so, he was beginning to worry about their safety here.

"What kind of jacking off you guys up to back there?"

McConnell looked indignant. "You know Bids. Fuckin' around. Stupid kid."

Keohane turned back toward the worksite. Sure enough, he saw Bids's head over the top of a half-demolished wall. Keohane took a few steps to the side and saw the kid was squatting over a small pile of concrete, pawing at it like a toddler in a sandbox. Keohane felt a short spike of anger that wasn't wholly unpleasant. Bids was Michael's age and Keohane liked to think if Michael was around, he'd be here in the asphalt and dust, tearing down with his dad, not acting like a dumb fuck who smoked too much weed and lived in his parents' basement. Michael was a smart kid, a fucking tough kid. It had come as a shock, but not a surprise when Keohane

205

woke one morning three years ago to an empty house, the emergency cash in the freezer disappeared along with his son. Mike wasn't a halfwit like Bids. He was out there surviving. Keohane clung to this as if it were truth.

"Bids!" The rest of the scattered crew turned at Keohane's heads-up, but Bids kept sifting. "Goddammit, it's too hot for this shit. Mick, stay here and stick your hand in the cooler for a few."

Keohane stalked over to Bids with his breath held, ready to bawl him out like a drill sergeant when he got there. But Bids didn't look up, just pointed at the rubble between his feet and said, "I found a hand."

Keohane pushed him to the side with a little more force than necessary and saw the bones, still half buried. They looked like the skeletal remains of a child's hand, the bones were so tiny and neat. Bids had cleared the concrete and broken brick from around it, but he wouldn't pick it up. Instead, he leaned over and blew hard on the thing, like he was putting out candles on a birthday cake.

Keohane crouched and touched the hand. It was cold, even in this heat. He couldn't say why, but he knew it wasn't human. Something about it was too neat, too graceful. It was almost pretty. A thing like that couldn't belong to a kid.

"What the fuck?"

Keohane and Bids jerked at the voice above them, but didn't respond. Nance squinted for a minute, stroking a scar above his left eyebrow.

"I was coming down through to the foundation there when I saw it," Bids said and moved back from the hand a little. Nance took the space for himself and bent toward the ground, curious. He was so tall and thin, Keohane wondered how he ever got close to anything at all. Now, as Nance stretched out one long arm toward the skeletal hand, Keohane was reminded of that old Italian painting, the famous one, God finger to finger with Adam.

"You find any more of it?" Nance asked, brushing the debris around it.

Bids went pale beneath his acne. "You think there's more?"

The rest of the crew had drifted in, drawn by the scene, silent as ghosts. Even McConnell had come over from the truck, his hand puckered and beaded with ice water. Keohane glanced from man to man. He knew he should say something. They were all on the clock and lunch wasn't for another half hour at least.

"'Kay, prairie dogs, back to work," Keohane chided them softly. No one moved. They were all watching Nance, strange Nance, who had, they'd heard, been a high school teacher, a ship's captain, a person of importance at MIT or some such place. No one could ever quite figure it out, and he wouldn't say. Would only answer, "I had one life, and then I had another." They were all a little afraid of him, but they wanted to know what his big brain was churning up. Silence encased them like the Garden itself, and the far-off swish of the traffic on 93 seemed to break and fade away. Nance carefully pried the hand from the hard dirt and brought it close to his face, squinting like a scholar. He nodded and cleared his throat. They all leaned in.

"Ooh," grunted Nance, hard and deep. "Ooh ooh." The men exchanged worried looks and Nance let out the throttle, his grunts transforming into ear-piercing shrieks. He jumped from one foot to the other and scratched his armpit with the skeleton hand, howling. Keohane thought Bids looked like he was about to turn tail and run home. Not that he blamed the kid; Keohane had the heebies too, and thought if Nance didn't shut the fuck up real fast, things were going to get ugly.

As if Keohane had spoken aloud, Nance stopped the screaming dance and grinned. "It's a monkey, you dumb fucks. A monkey hand." He tossed it at Bids, who gasped and almost fell backwards into the brick dust when it hit his chest.

"Freak," Bids mumbled, and wandered off to his jackhammer a few yards away, finished with the whole scene.

The other guys followed, except for McConnell, who wouldn't return to work today and probably not tomorrow either.

"How'd you figure that, Nance?"

Nance picked up the hand and pointed at the dirty bones. "See how the thumb's as long as the fingers? A kid's hand, or even a midget's, would have short fingers and a small palm."

When Nance didn't go on, Keohane fed him the question he was waiting for. "All right then, how the fuck did a monkey hand end up here?" Keohane gestured at the sweating blacktop streets that surrounded them. The hollow clang of Bids's jackhammer threw up a swarm of fat pigeons at the other end of the parking lot. It cut through the white surging noise of the traffic entering and exiting, made it seem to vibrate in kind.

"The circus, buddy. You remember? Barnum and Bailey and their alabaster unicorn."

McConnell laughed, "I told my sister it was a goat. You should have heard that kid howl."

"Yeah, sure," said Keohane, "cotton candy, flaming hoops, lion tamers—"

"Remember, on the fairway, they'd display the animals before the barker came out, so you could get a real look at the tigers' claws, or see how the unicorn wasn't just some messed-up horse with a paper horn stapled to its head?"

209

"I used to throw peanuts at 'em," said McConnell, and Keohane told him he was pretty sure McConnell had been in one of them cages, and Nance said, "Sure he was, right in there with the jumping poodles. Isn't that right? With the fancy hair and sparkly skirts?"

McConnell didn't laugh this time, but said, "Ah," and walked back to the truck to ice his hand some more.

Nance gestured away from them, "The trolley car where the monkeys were kept would have been back over there, around gate C. The last time I went—what was that, twelve years ago? thirteen?—the cages were all blocked off. They'd lost one. I remember all the posters around town about it."

"Sure," Keohane said. "This old mop man on our block used to complain about finding shit on the basketball court, garbage cans knocked around. He swore something was watching him. Something evil, he used to say." Keohane laughed. "Everybody thought it was bullshit."

Nance touched the paw in his hand. "It's like that old story. You know, the one where the man finds a monkey's paw that grants wishes, but the wishes come out all twisted. Like the dad wishes for money, and he gets it when his son dies. Then he wishes for his son to come back, and there's a knock on the door, but his son had been mutilated and buried over a week ago, and the dad thinks whatever's on the other side of the door will probably drive him insane to look at, so with the last wish, he wishes the boy dead again."

Keohane's mouth was dry. He thought the father in the story a terrible fool, but he didn't say this aloud.

Later, Keohane and Nance sat in baking, broken arena seats beneath a tree near a section of sidewalk. They ate the tunafish and rye sandwiches that Keohane had made the night before.

"I forgot about that story—about the monkey in the Garden. Some kid, my boy's friend when he was little… what was that kid's name? Anyway, this kid claimed he saw that monkey at a Celtics game one time. Forgot about that too. Makes me feel bad about tearing the old place down." Keohane took a bite of sandwich and let his gaze wander over the brick and steel wreck his crew had patiently wrought. "I always liked the tightrope walkers. You know? Up there like they weigh nothing."

Nance paused for a minute, then spoke quietly: "I never knew you had a son."

Keohane blinked and wiped his hands on his pants. "He's been gone for a while now. Ran away a few years ago." Nance raised his head to the sun and shut his eyes, a man lost for a moment in the persistent ache of his own memories. "He sure hated those goddamned animals though. Just started screaming every time we got near the lion cages."

Nance smiled and took another bite of his sandwich. He had set the skeleton hand between them, palm up, as if it were begging. "Goddamned wall monkey. Between the peanuts and popcorn and the hot dogs and beer, he had it pretty good, I guess."

Keohane nodded. It was one of those goddamned things for sure.

They watched Bids work on what was left of a structure-bearing wall in the distance. The chunky jackhammer rap, the heat, and food made Keohane feel trancy. He watched the last of the Garden come down and remembered the smells: peanut oil and the shit of fierce animals. And Michael, so deliciously afraid. He remembered the rubber-and-popcorn stink of Michael's tennis shoes, remembered standing stacked in the audience for what seemed like hours, Michael's legs straddling his aching neck, his boy's arms outstretched as if to catch the acrobats that fell toward them like light.

Curse or no curse, Keohane thought, he would take his son back in a heartbeat. Dead or rotting or torn apart. That was the selfish weight of a father's true love. No matter what, he would've opened that door.

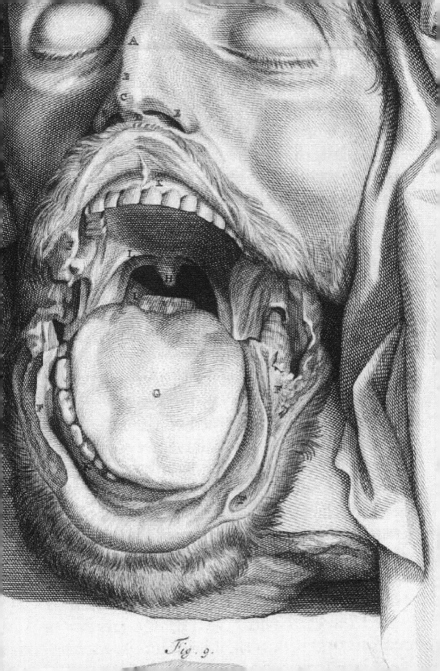

Fig. 9.

HOMEWORK

1. Autobiography

Daniel Robert Cooley is 14. He wants to be a Bull Rider when he grows up. This is his favorite joke: "How do you get a dog to stop humping your leg? Suck his dick."

2. Lunch

The mural on the north side of the cafeteria is so ugly. He doesn't know if it's ugly because it's ugly, or if it's ugly because he stares at it every day for sixteen minutes, which is how long it takes him to eat through the little squared-off portions in his lunch tray at his assigned seat in the cafeteria. He doesn't taste the food as much if he stares at the mural, but the mural sometimes makes him as sick as the food. He's never quite understood how the mural could've got there. It looks like the work of kindergarteners, with a wavering, green landscape of hills and trees, and lumpy, multicolored children holding hands, smiling broad faced. But this is a middle school and it's an embarrassment.

He suspects it may have been painted by the retards, who burp and moan at the other end of his table. He accidentally looks toward them and makes eye contact with Leroy, who's staring at him as usual from the opposite bench six feet away. He turns back to the mural, but it's too late.

"D.R.! Hi, D.R.!" Leroy yells and scoots backwards down the bench like an inchworm in reverse. He pushes off with the soft rubber heels of his tennis shoes until his legs are straight, then he draws his knees up to his chest and pushes off again. It takes him three scoots before he is sitting straight across from D.R., blocking his view of the ugliest mural in the world. "Hi, D.R. Hey, D.R. Hi."

"I heard you the first time," D.R. says through a mouthful of square pizza.

"Whatcha eatin', D.R.?" Leroy leans so close to his food that D.R. has to slide the tray away before Leroy's nose ends up in his steamed carrots.

"Get your germs away from my food."

Leroy sits back up, smiling and obedient. "What is it, D.R.?"

216

"What do you mean, 'What is it?' It's the same thing you ate, you stupid retard. Everybody here is eating the same thing."

Leroy laughs as if D.R. has just told the funniest joke.

The other retards are looking at them now, judging the safety of the situation. Any minute they would all come over and surround him with their frog-eyed faces.

D.R. clears his throat. "Hey, Leroy, do you know what's better than being in the Special Olympics?" Leroy opens his mouth wide and wags his head back and forth. "Not being a retard. Now leave me alone."

Leroy is still smiling with his mouth, but the eyes dart back and forth, avoiding him. D.R. shoves the carrots into his mouth in two big bites and gets up, still chewing, to dump his tray. On his way to the wastebaskets, Andy Herkness sticks a huge, muddy boot into his path. D.R. steps around it.

"How are your friends, D.R.? Looks like you were havin' yourself a good old time at the tard table." Andy sits by himself, but two girls at the opposite end of his table look up. One of them, a ninth-grader named Karen, meets D.R.'s eyes and smiles a quiet smile from underneath a flip of smooth, blond hair. She volunteers at the hospital gift shop, where D.R. has bought plastic army men and Ertl trucks from her to give to Marshall after chemo. He's never spoken to her at school. He senses that this would not be an okay thing to do. Karen turns back to her friend and D.R.'s ears get hot as Andy tosses a carrot at him. "Tard lover. I'm talking to you."

Andy has assigned seating for throwing a chair at Mrs.

Peterson when she was in the middle of reading "Romeo and Juliet: Abridged" from the *World Classics Made Easy* textbook. Andy is sixteen years old. He has a lip-smudge mustache and violence comes off him like a smell.

The bell rings, so D.R. has an excuse to ignore Andy. He looks back at the table, but Karen is already walking away. Later, he will absentmindedly draw the stitching from the back pocket of her designer jeans in his Pre-Algebra notebook. He goes out the rear of the cafeteria through the kitchen door to have a smoke and cut fourth period.

3. Parent-Teacher Conference

Betty is elbow-deep in Shake 'n' Bake when the phone rings. She sighs mightily and throws the bag of chicken and chalky breading into the sink, where it raises a small cloud that dusts the faucet tap. In her opinion, nobody bothered calling unless they wanted something. Good news and gossip traveled the grapevine, but favors and bills were called in. Lately, the hospital had been especially busy on her line. The insurance company too. And they'd taken a second mortgage for Marshall's new treatments. Surely, the bank was closed at this hour.

"Yeah?" Betty grips the phone and sets her jaw.

"Mrs. Cooley?"

"Yep."

"Hi, Mrs. Cooley, I'm Rhonda Petersen, Daniel's English teacher?"

Betty rolls her eyes at sound of the young, pretty voice and doesn't speak.

"Hi. Um...Mrs. Cooley—"

"You can call me Betty, Rhonda." Betty wonders who would name their child Rhonda. No one famous or good has ever been called Rhonda.

"Oh." A titter. "That's kind of you, um, Betty."

"Rhonda, how can I help you? Supper's just about fixed and I got some hungry men to feed."

"Oh, sure, of course. I'm very sorry to interrupt, but..." Rhonda clears her throat. "Well, I couldn't help but notice that you and Mr. Cooley—"

"Bill." Betty enjoys the beat of timid silence on the line.

"Right. Bill. Well, you and Bill weren't at Daniel's parent—"

"D.R." Betty smiles and traces a little circle on the side table with a breaded finger.

"I'm sorry?" Rhonda's voice is tight and high. Betty imagines her turning red and fidgeting with the coils of her office telephone cord.

"He's D.R. That's what his family calls him. That's what his friends call him. That's what he prefers."

Rhonda sighs sharp and fast. The silence that follows is longer this time. "Mrs.—Betty, if I've called at a bad time..."

"Time's fine. Like I told you, I just got to finish the supper in a minute, so..."

"Well," Rhonda clears her throat again. "I didn't get a chance to talk to you and your husband at the parent-teacher conferences on Tuesday." She pauses, then continues. "And I have some concerns about—"

"We weren't there is why you didn't see us. D.R. didn't tell us about any conference." Betty frowns and looks around as if to confirm this with the hallway.

"I just need to let you know that D.R. is going to fail English this semester if he doesn't start applying himself." Rhonda's voice grows louder with conviction. "He wrote a very...well, I gave this assignment in class. The students were supposed to write a short essay about themselves. Like a biography, like authors have in books, you know?"

"And you failed him? Why would he write a biography if he ain't even wrote a book yet, Rhonda?" Betty is suddenly very angry at this woman and her silly assignment. Like all the other yo-yos at the school, this woman wants to make her son feel stupid and small.

"Betty, that's what I'm trying to say. He did write it. He wrote the biography. May I read it to you?"

"Sure, Rhonda."

"Fine. This is what your son wrote in my class yesterday. 'Daniel Robert Cooley is fourteen. He wants to be a bull rider. This is his favorite joke: How do you get a dog to stop... um...humping your leg?" She exhales through her nose, into the receiver, and breathes in again, as if for strength. "Suck his..." She ends on a high and pleading note.

"Suck his what, Rhonda?" Betty's face is nearly split in two by a grin.

"Mrs. Cooley," Rhonda warbles. "I'm sure you can figure it out."

"Rhonda, if I don't even know what you think D.R. did wrong, then how am I supposed to make it right? Why have you even called me? And in the middle of dinner?" Betty's voice has risen too. A small snort escapes her.

"Dick, Mrs. Cooley! Suck his dick! Your son wrote Suck. His. Dick! In my classroom!"

Betty cannot, does not want to, stop the bray that bursts from her open mouth. She laughs and laughs, hunches forward and laughs some more. That joke got her every time, but this was by far the funniest it had ever been. She laughs through Rhonda's terse goodbye, holding the phone to her big belly like a friend. She is nearly doubled over when Bill steps into the hallway from the living room, a look of worry on his face.

"What's going on, Betty? Sounds like you're having a coronary."

Betty is only able to squeak out "Suck his dick," before she is roaring again.

Bill breaks into a cautious smile, "What?"

Betty straightens up, sighs, "Ah," and wipes her eyes with the back of her wrist before putting the telephone back in its cradle. Really, D.R. was one smart cookie, if you thought about it.

4. Math—Extra Credit

Q. All six members of The Dave Matthews Band (the singer, the drummer, the bass player, the guitarist, the saxophonist, and the violinist) are trying to cross the Cedar River to get to the big concert at The Three Seasons Coliseum in Cedar Valley. Only two people can be in the boat at a time or it will sink. Dave and the drummer don't know how to row a boat. At any time, in the boat, the number of band members who play stringed instruments must be greater than or equal to the number of band members who play other instruments. In what combination do they take the ferry?

A: Cal Tippwater is the fastest calf-roper in the First Frontier Pro-Rodeo Circuit. He can rope a calf in under 7.2 seconds. Cal is on his way to the Summer Stampede at the Sweet River Arena in Ketona. Cal stops his truck to take a leak and there's The Dave Matthews Band by the river. Cal ropes the whole band together and puts them in the boat and the boat sinks. The mayor of Cedar Valley gives Cal a key to the city and says thanks for saving our town from the most godawful shit music we ever heard. The end.

5. A Letter

Dear Tommy Janes,

My name is Marshall Cooley and I think you are the best bull rider in the world. My brother his name is D.R. Cooley and he likes you too. But he likes Cal Tippwater too but Cal is a calf-roper. Are you friends with Cal? My brother D.R. says he bets you won't read this letter cause of you're famous. I hope you read it. My brother D.R. is going to be a bull rider when he grows up. My brother D.R. asked me if I want to be a bull rider when I grow up. I told him "Does a bear shit in the woods?" My brother D.R. told me that joke when I was little. My brother D.R. tells me lots of jokes. That is my favorite joke he told me. What is your favorite joke? I am writing you a letter because I am going to see you at the rodeo next week. I don't know if

223

I will get to be a bull rider for real.

> *Your Friend,*
> *Marshall Cooley*

6. Rodeo

We're all at the rodeo tonight because my little brother, Marshall, is sick and will probably be dead pretty soon. He's been on chemo and in the hospital on and off for a long time, since I was in fifth grade. It must be getting bad though, because he only goes in for treatments once a week now, and any dumbass can tell he's not getting better.

When rodeo tickets came in the mail from Wishes Come True, I knew he was a goner. Mom and Dad told him it was a Christmas present to all of us from Santa, but I saw the letter in the garbage after dinner. Marshall acted so happy, but I bet he knew something funny was going on. He told me last Christmas he knew there wasn't any Santa Claus, but I shouldn't tell Mom and Dad because they might get mad. So there we were, all sitting around eating franks and beans, lying to each other like strangers.

Still, I'd be a bigger liar if I said I wish I wasn't here. This isn't my first time at a rodeo. I been to small ones up in Pleasant Hill and Waylen. A lot of towns in Iowa are on different circuits, so in the summer you can drive to a whole new rodeo every weekend. But they're all pretty pissant, with nobody famous and sometimes no bull riding at all. I don't understand how you can even call it a rodeo if there's no bull riding. It should be illegal. Like false advertising or something. One time, me and my dad and brother drove all the way to New Town just to see this show that looked pretty good. Travis Tritt was supposed to play some songs and it said Tommy Janes was going to be there. Tommy Janes is one of the best bull riders ever and I couldn't wait to see him pull a line, except when we got there the whole stupid rodeo was only a little bit of dirt and a fence in some crappy old armory on the edge of town. Tommy Janes was there but all he did was introduce Travis, who played one lousy song and then they both disappeared and we sat there watching some cowboys in fancy hats twirl ropes around in the dirt for an hour. Then Marshall puked up this red stuff that looked like Kool-Aid and we all just gave up and went home.

This time it's the big one. Everybody famous is going to be there since it's an off-season exhibition and they don't have anywhere else to be yet. We drove down to Kansas City last night and checked into our hotel, which is right in the middle of the fancy part of town, which you can tell is the fancy

225

part of town from the old-fashioned street lights and how the restaurants and stores all have clean awnings that match. I guess the hotel is free too, because Mom kept touching things—the bathroom countertop, the crinkled lampshade on the table between our two huge beds, the little shampoos and soaps—and telling Dad in a whispery, excited voice how we could never afford to stay here. Dad frowned and went out to find the ice machine for his beer.

When we get to the rodeo, we have to park way in the back lot, which is so far away from the arena that Marshall gets tired just on the way to the main gate and Dad has to give him a piggyback. Inside, Mom keeps staring at girls in tight T-shirts that stop above their belly buttons. She mutters "Jesus" when we pass by a lady wearing a jeans skirt so short I can almost see her underwear. "In March, too. Who can dress like that?" She frowns and swears at the sawdust on the ground. I stick close by her to try and get a better look at the slutty ones. I think Dad's doing the same thing I am, because Marshall keeps yelling at him to stop jerking his head around so much. By the time we get to our seats, Mom is spitting mad and I've got a boner and Dad has already smacked Marshall for being bossy. We're all glad when the lights go down.

There's some drill team crap by pansies riding horses and wearing shiny blue chaps, and the rodeo clowns run around in

226

the empty ring and smash pies into each other's faces, which is pretty dumb, but the little kids seem to like it, even Marshall, who is only nine but sometimes seems older, probably just because he can't run around and make as much noise as other little kids, since he's so tired all the time. Then the bull riders come out. They wear chaps too, but theirs are regular colors, and dusty, like they already been tossed a couple times. They make a walking ring around the arena, so everybody can get a good look at them. The loudspeaker announces their names, and they wave or put their thumbs in the air, and everyone screams for their favorites. When the announcer says, "Number 23, Tommy Janes from Tulsa, Oklahoma," me and my brother start yelling. We stand up and jump up and down (which I can do because my boner's been gone since the clowns), but we can't even hear ourselves the cheering's so loud for Tommy. The riders go back to the pens and it's on. Everybody's stomping and hollering and getting rowdy like every ride is the last ride they'll ever see. It's a beautiful thing for sure, but Tommy's down the whole time, until the end of the second round, when he makes the bell, and I notice that some girl a couple rows down and to the side of us has these huge boobs that are bouncing as she claps and jumps, and that's a beautiful thing too. Boner city again.

Between riding rounds, they have the calf-roping

competition. Some people think it's baby stuff, and I notice a bunch of them leaving their seats to take a leak or get more beer or whatever, but Cal Tippwater's the main contender, and I never seen him in real life. He's so fast, you can't believe it. Like a magician or something, but he's actually doing what you think he's doing, which is roping a calf so quick you could miss it if you blink or look over to check the boobs on the girl in front of you. So when Marshall says he wants to go down to the pens to get Tommy Janes's autograph, I pretend like I don't hear him and hoot over his whiny voice when they announce Cal. Dad taps me hard on the shoulder and leans over so his arm is around me, and Marshall is between us, getting squished and saying "Ow" over and over again.

"Did you hear your brother?" he asks and tugs hard on my ear.

"Christ!" I yell and rub my ear.

"Don't you swear at me. You heard him: take him down to the pens." Dad sits back, going for the beer resting in his crotch.

"I'm watching Cal," I say, itching to slap Marshall, who's already shoving past all the jutting knees to the aisle. Dad reaches for my ear again. I stand up and stick my thumbs through my belt loops so my hands kind of cover my junk, which is not quite back to normal.

"That fucker," I say quietly when I get to the aisle. Marshall doesn't say anything. I know he won't tell. He's not that kind of kid. Instead, we march single file down the stairs until we're at floor level.

He says, "You can stay here and watch the ropers, I'm gonna go 'round over there." He points to a line of kids holding programs, and I can see Tommy Janes at the head of it with his hat tilted down, scribbling autographs. I watch Marshall walk for a few seconds, until a couple of bigger kids point at his chick-fuzzed head, and I turn back to the ring. When I do, the boob girl is standing right beside me.

"Hi," she says, and snaps her gum and smiles. She's younger than I thought, not much older than me probably. Her T-shirt says, *2002 Huntsville Rodeo: Best of the West*, and I pretend to read it.

"Up here, dummy," she says, still smiling. I look at her face, which is okay, with a couple of zits and weird frosted lips, but a nice nose.

"I'm D.R."

"Hi, D.R., I'm Grace. What're you doin' down here?"

I want to look at her boobs again, but instead I turn back to the line of kids in front of Tommy. "My little brother's getting Tommy Janes's autograph."

"Which one's he?"

229

"The tall guy with the number on his back."

Grace giggles and smacks her gum. "No, dummy, which one's your little brother?"

I point and she steps closer so her right boob is brushing my arm. My boner starts to crank and I put a hand in my pocket. "Uh, he's that one, with the...in the orange shirt."

"Oh," she says kind of funny and doesn't say anything else for a second. Then she steps back. "What's wrong with his hair?"

"Well, he's...it's growing back." My face gets hot. I hope she stops talking.

"Did he shave it off?"

"No." I try to turn back to watch the ropers, but Grace is by my side, still staring past me at my brother.

"Does he have cancer or something?"

"Yeah," I say without looking at her, but she just keeps staring. My boner's deflating. I take my hand out of my pocket.

Two girls come up behind Grace. They're both skinny, and they don't have boobs. One of them looks mean, with a tight mouth and blond hairsprayed bangs. She puts her arm around Grace's neck. "Hey, girl. Who're you talking to?"

"Check it out. That kid over there has cancer. It's his brother."

The girls look at me, then stretch their necks out, and Tight Mouth says, "No shit?"

"Hey," I say. I have to say it twice because now they're all staring at my brother like he's a fucking freak or something. When they turn back to me, I tell the joke I heard Herkness telling over and over again at lunch the other day. "What's the difference between a blond and a mosquito?" Their eyes all get big at the same time, like they had practiced it or something. "One stops sucking when you slap it."

Then I walk away, Grace going, "I don't get it," and Tight Mouth starting to yell something about getting her brother, but the announcer comes over the PA with the final roping scores and the crowd's going nuts again. I get to Marshall, who shows me his signed program, which says, "Shoot for the stars, Marshel."

He shrugs and says, "Oh well. Least Cal set the circuit record. You seen that just now?"

I nod and say, "Yeah, it was pretty cool. Let's go up on this side. I gotta take a piss."

7. Reproduction Unit

As Mr. Davis calls out each assigned couple, the groans and titters grow louder. Beneath the noise, D.R. repeats to himself the names of the cute girls in his class—Jenny, Dory, Lynn, Jenny, Trish—over and over until, with a surge of excitement and despair, he hears his name.

"Daniel Cooley, Marcia Dalton."

His stomach drops a little. Marcia's not cute, but she's not totally awful either. She's quiet and nice and she always gets good grades, which he could definitely use, so this isn't a total wash. He whispers, "Not a wash," a few times to calm himself down, then cracks up when Jason gets put with Denise. Denise has got to be two-hundred pounds if she's anything and no one in his right mind would try and knock her up. D.R. turns around and points at Jason and smacks his desk, like he's just heard a humdinger. Mr. Davis is staring him down when he faces front again. He smiles nonchalantly and winks back at Jason, who is throwing him a low middle finger.

"Mr. Cooley, perhaps you'd like to start us off then?" Davis points to the basket of hard-boiled eggs on his desk. "Come up and claim your baby."

D.R. crosses his arms. "It's not mine, Mr. Davis." The class busts out all over again.

Mr. Davis smirks. "I'm sure you'll have plenty of opportunities in the future to practice that line. For now, why don't you humor us."

D.R. mumbles "Dick," but gets up and grabs an egg.

232

It's smooth as river-washed stone, which surprises him. It's not like he's never held an egg before. Hell, he's held lots of them, just before launching them onto car windows and vinyl siding, for example. But here, in General Health class, in front of Davis, the egg is a strange thing in his hand. For a weird, stupid second, he's terrified he'll drop it. He turns it over and sees that Mr. Davis has gifted it with a face. The egg squints and frowns in permanent marker. D.R. props it in the pencil-holder space on his desk while Mr. Davis blah-blahs on about responsibility and making family dates with your unit partners.

D.R. looks sideways at Marcia and decides that she's not so uncute as he'd always thought. She has long eyelashes and a pretty, ski-slope nose, even if she is kind of chubby. The idea of spending some time alone in his basement with her isn't looking so bad.

"The egg is yours for one week," Mr. Davis finishes as the last couple retrieves its egg cautiously. "A broken egg, even just a cracked shell, will get you an F for this project." The bell rings. "By the way, people, my wife drew those faces. She can spot an imposter from a mile away."

D.R. gets up to meet Jason at the door and bust his balls a little, but Marcia steps in front of him. "Why don't I take it, all right? I'll give it back tomorrow and we can just take

233

turns like that. You don't need to come over to my house or anything. And you better not break it, okay? Please, don't ruin this grade for me." Marcia looks like she might slap him, or cry. She also looks a lot like their baby, her face kind of scrunched and turned down, like someone has drawn it on wrong.

"What the hell?" D.R. puts the hand with the egg in it behind his back. He no longer wants to be alone with her in any room, least of all this one. "It's mine too. I'll give it to you after school." He tries to walk around her but she steps with him and crosses her arms.

"No. What lunch period do you have? I'll get it then."

"I'm going to lunch now. You can have it after," he says, and gives the egg a little toss as he brushes by her.

Jason is waiting outside the classroom door. "What was that all about?" he asks.

D.R. shakes his head. "I don't know. I thought she was supposed to be nice."

Jason shrugs and grabs at the egg. "Let me see it."

"Fuck off, where's your egg?" He doesn't say anything and D.R. laughs, "Obese Denise? What a fine piece of ass." D.R. kisses the air as Jason does an about-face and walks away.

The cafeteria is the usual scene. Out of the lunch line, D.R. takes the long way around the table to avoid the retards, who seem to be, momentarily at least, interested in their own silly dramas. He sets the egg in a bed of creamed corn on his tray. Its mouth is open and showing a single tooth under a pair of crying eyes. He taps the shiny, bald head of it lightly with his fingernail, and the shell seems to shiver over the soft mass inside. D.R. looks up from the egg to where the mural smiles across the wall, all badly drawn children and sunshine forest. He sighs and turns the egg toward the mural.

"It's okay," he whispers. "You never really had a chance." There is a sharp crack as he brings the spoon down. The shell splinters over a thin film that he peels away like sunburned skin.

8. Friends

The retards are out at the buses behind the school on Monday, milling and quacking. D.R. wonders briefly what's going on, since they're usually let out a half hour before everyone else. He walks to his spot, behind a small utility shed, to smoke before his bus shows up, keeping a lookout for Jason, who may or may not be mad at him. But Herkness is already there, sitting and laughing like an idiot with a small, mean boy named Jim. Jim's got a can of spray paint between his legs and a streak of brown around his lips that D.R. thinks

235

goes pretty good with his shit-eating grin. D.R. does a 180 and begins to walk away, but they've already seen him.

"Hey fucker!" Andy yells and Jim giggles like a girl. "Come back here, tard lover."

D.R. turns around but doesn't move.

"I said, come over here. I want to knock your fucking head in!"

Jim laughs again and takes a pull at the can, coughing and falling back against the shed with a tinny boom.

"No thanks, Jerkness."

Andy tries to stand up, but the fumes have made him dizzy. He slumps back down. "You better not tell on us, or you're dead, man."

D.R. tries to unclench his jaw and fists, which have bunched not so much with anger as with fear, even though Andy's too far away and fucked up to do any damage today. "School's out. You don't need my help to get caught." D.R. turns around and runs right into Leroy, whose big, soft body gives like a pillow.

"D.R.! Hi! Hey, D.R., guess what?" Leroy's stupid face is an inch from his, breathing a wet, sour wind right up his nose. He hears Jim dumbcroaking again behind him and pushes Leroy away.

"Christ, get out of my face, Leroy."

"Guess what, D.R.?" Leroy has a hand up his shirt, and is rubbing at his chest excitedly. "Guess what? Our bus got into a big wreck! A big wreck and he can't come pick us up today." D.R. nods and starts to walk away when he hears Herkness yell, "Leroy! Main man Leroy. Come here! I got something to show you." His voice is high-pitched and jovial. Leroy jogs to the shed like a happy dog.

D.R. sighs and calls out, "Leroy! Get back over here," but the boy is already caught up in the kind mystery Herkness seems prepared to offer. When D.R. gets to the shed, Andy is standing with his hands cupped around Leroy's nose and mouth, the can sticking out between his palms like a metal snout.

"Just like that, okay? Now take a big breath in when I— fuck!" Andy drops the can and smacks Leroy hard in the back of the head as D.R. approaches. "Stop getting your retard slobber all over me!" Leroy crumples forward onto his knees, his mouth open but no sound coming out.

D.R. covers the last three feet of asphalt with a long step and a roundhouse punch that gets Andy hard on the cheek. He stumbles, but comes back, bent over, and plants his head in D.R.'s gut. Both of them go to the ground and D.R.'s insides slam together. His own wide-mouthed rasp fills his ears as he struggles to breathe, and Andy's fist connects with

237

his upper teeth.

Andy yells and jumps back, holding his hand, and D.R. rolls over to vomit, his mouth hot and full of their blood. His spine tingles in expectation of the boot that doesn't come. He looks up from his pile, which reminds him of Marshall's puke at New Town, and begins to cry as he sees Mr. Chaney, the burly tard-minder, pinning Andy against the wall of the school.

9. Out-of-School Suspension

It's not very late, so the side door to the school's still unlocked, but since it's Friday, there's nobody here but one janitor up on the second floor. I checked it all out soon as I got here. I brought my backpack to make it look like I was on official business and I practiced my cover story, which is that I forgot a book from my locker. I even hid my bike in the bushes under Mrs. Peterson's room to be extra safe, and put on my sneakers, which I figured out this week, with so much time on my hands to think, are called sneakers for a good reason. But I didn't see nobody, except for that one janitor, who seemed happy enough with his earbuds and his tile buffer, and didn't even notice me peeking around a corner to check him out.

Marshall's been in the hospital since Tuesday and Mom and Dad been there almost straight, just back home a couple times to give me lunch and dinner. They didn't say nothing about the fight, so I guess Marsh is in bad shape. Dad said he'll pick me up tonight around eight to go see him, so I'm clear until then.

I go as quiet as I can up the main hall to the cafeteria, running my tongue over my chipped front tooth, which I been doing a lot this week, sitting there in front of all the dumb homework my teachers sent over. I wouldn't have even opened up the packet, except for I got so bored. I hate soap operas and game shows and all that was on the country channel was NASCAR racing, and with Marshall in the hospital, I didn't really feel like doing anything fun anyways.

The ball in the can of spray paint rattles in my backpack and I freeze for a second, but the tile buffer's still mowing away up there, so I keep going and open the cafeteria door just enough to slip through. Only two of the overhead lights are on, but it's enough to see by. Not like anybody would ever miss that fucking mural anyway.

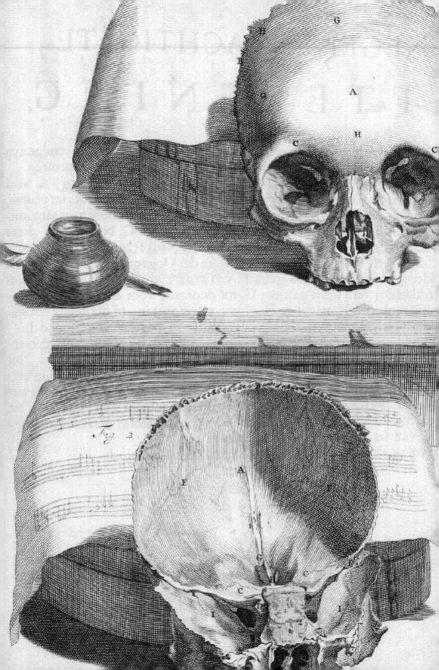

Fig. 2.

ANAMNESIS: AN EPILOGUE

Hepatitis A, hepatitis B, mumps/measles/rubella, polio, yellow fever, influenza (semi-annually), typhoid

Untimely death of mother, macular degeneration, Alzheimer's, stroke-related dementia, stomach cancer, immolation, airplane crash, quadriplegia, loneliness

Multiple incorrect self-diagnoses including: malaria, cancer, blood clot, bipolar disorder, color blindness, Celiac disease, seasonal affective disorder, diabetes type II, carpal tunnel syndrome, tetanus

Worked in food service while suffering from mononucleosis (1998: Perkins Family Restaurant store MADISON II, 1410 Damon Road, Madison, WI)

Naproxen sodium (2200mg), ibuprofen (2000mg), escitalopram oxalate (1330mg), sildenafil citrate (500mg), varenicline tartrate (17mg), lorazepam (12.5mg), clonazepam (5mg)

General hygiene average-to-good, dependent upon workload, relationship status

Increase in stress and concurrent cigarette smoking results in recent weight fluctuations. Prognosis: purchase of tighter jeans, slightly shorter skirts

Consistently underhydrated

Walgreen's brand "Scar Gel" applied negligently. All scars still present

Atypically anallergic to plants in the Anacardiaceae family

Childhood eczema

Family history of psoriasis: not inherited

Monthlong full-body outbreak of hives in college misdiagnosed as syphilis, as yet unexplained

Tattooed with Starbrite Black Outlining Ink (may include iron oxide, carbon, and logwood extract), age 28. Psychological status leading to tattoo acquisition—chronic. Times New Roman font—already faded

Two pennies removed from left nostril at age 2 by steady-handed, mustachioed pediatrician

Head lice (age 9) leads to preference for mentholated shampoos

Tongue bit through in gym class, age 7, healed one month later; tongue pierced at age 19 (Hall Mall complex, Iowa City, IA), healed one week after removal, age 23

Despite early fluoridation efforts, six cement-filled cavities

Eyes: relatively flat, "football" shaped
High risk of retinal detachment
Corneas: heartbreakingly thin

One year of counseling following parents' divorce

Hormonal cystic acne treated with Retin-A, Retin-A Micro, Aloe Vera gel (CVS brand), benzoyl peroxide (2.5%), salicylic acid (1.5%), toothpaste (Classic Crest®), human tears

"Brain shudders" caused by Lexapro withdrawal, not unpleasant

Occupational use of cocaine while waitressing

Chin stitches at Bellevue ER while seated next to patient under influence of crystalline methamphetamine hydrochloride. Status of patient's left testicle and upper thigh after staple removal: unknown

Removal of chin stitches: average cost of $28 per second

Recurrance of dream about being set on fire by masked stranger diminishing in frequency with age

Imitrex for migraine headaches may worsen pre-existing anxiety disorder

Three concussions

Temporomandibular joint disorder weakening jaw structure, increasing likelihood of dislocation and future dysfunction. Surgical correction likely to be necessary within 10 years

Wisdom tooth extraction: first introduction to benzodiazepines (and benzodiazepine derivatives); beginning of long, fruitful relationship

Hands of ex-boyfriend cause slight tracheal damage but produce no bruises to photograph

Regulated breathing during scuba diving, snorkeling, and some types of yoga may trigger feelings of claustrophobia/ exacerbate pre-existing anxiety disorder

Chantix for three months, enough to quit smoking for eight

Move from sea level to 4,226 feet, age 31: lung capacity diminished

Greater than average risk for myocardial infarction could lead to scar formations in heart

Moderate Paroxysmal Atrial Tachycardia (inherited) episodes marked by extremely rapid heartbeat due to a "short circuit" in electrical system. Breathtaking, but not life–threatening

One failed relationship ending in death

Potential for breast cancer: better than average (maternal history)

Love of own pets occasionally experienced as stomach pain

Swings taken at men other than father: 2

Student health IV–drip for drug–related dehydration unexpectedly comforting

Thumb (right) nearly split with handsaw while unsupervised (YMCA Camp Wapsie, Coggon, IA); recovered full function

Tip of index finger (left) nearly severed in metal fire door (Cambridge, MA); recovered full function

Tip of index finger (right) rat-bitten while intoxicated; recovered full function

Recent dog bite on knee (left) treated with Augmentin for 10 days. Relationship with dog tentatively optimistic

Hallux valgus tendencies in bones of both big toes. Probable surgical correction necessary by late fifties

Fifth toe (left) broken during drinking game (regionally known as "Beirut;" identical to nationally recognized "Beer Pong"). Never set

Semi-annual pedicures increase risk of fungal infections, prettiness

Evangelical church camp (age 8) causes temporary excess of sexual guilt/body shame; permanent avoidance of Bon Jovi

Frequency of masturbation: too often or not often enough dependent upon time of year and status of rechargeable batteries

Average number of new sexual partners per year decreasing steadily since age 26

Human papilloma virus
  Point of infection: Bipolar musician
  Treatments: cryotherapy, cervical colposcopy
  Cancer risk: moderate-high
  No scarring

Negative for syphilis when tested

Negative for gonorrhea when tested

Negative for chlamydia when tested

Negative for herpes simplex II when tested

Negative for hepatitis C when tested

Negative for HIV when tested

Negative for pregnancy when tested

Negative for bipolar disorder when tested

Negative of evidence, an experiment, the results of a test, etc.: providing no support for a particular hypothesis; indicating the absence or non-existence of a specified substance not exhibiting evidence of the presence of

[Scar from Greek *eschara*—place of fire

To scarify to scratch to make incisions to wound to subject to merciless criticism

to make incisions in the bark of to anoint

To make] a road

ACKNOWLEDGMENTS

A huge thank you to Carissa Halston and Randolph Pfaff, whose passion, vision, dedication, and friendship made this book.

Thank you to my workshop leaders, professors, and mentors. At Vermont: Doug Glover, David Jauss, Chris Noël, Domenic Stansberry, and Nance van Winckel. At Utah: François Camoin, Joe Metz, Matt Potolsky, and Paisley Rekdal. Scott Black, Lance Olsen, and Melanie Rae Thon, you showed me the way.

Friends and colleagues, thank you for your support and love through the years: Xhenet Aliu, Geoffrey Babbitt, Scott Bartos, Josh Bell, Sean Boarini, Jeremy Brown, Danielle Cadena Deulen, Neal Carroll, Carrie Collier, Hope Coppinger, Kathryn Cowles, Raphael Dagold, Barbara Duffey, Emily Dyer, Andy Farnsworth, Robert Glick, Rachel Hanson, Kate Harding, Meg Harris, Will Kaufman, Esther Lee, Nate Liederbach, Rebecca Lindenberg, Steve Lindstrom,

Dawn Lonsinger, Rachel Marston, Tasha Matsumoto, Shena McAuliffe, Ben Miller, Angela Muzzarelli, Cami Nelson, John Nieves, Tim O'Keefe, Ryan O'Leary, Jacob Paul, Chris Perri, Natanya Pulley, Erin Rogers, Camie Schaefer, Dave Siegel, Bruce Stone, Janaka Stucky, Barbara Verchot, and Valerie Wetlaufer, and the amazing folks with whom I spent time at Vermont College, the University of Utah, and VCCA.

Sincere gratitude to muses Bowe, Duncan, and Ethan; big old retro shout-outs to 153 W. 80th St. and Lowell House. And "Once More, with Feeling"—Natanya Pulley.

Joe Keohane, Jen Sheldon, and Carolyn Sivitz: You helped me keep the faith.

Many thanks to the dedicated journal editors who first published the stories in this book.

Thank you Mom, Dad, Jenny and Marshall, and my bonus parents, Deb, Jim, Bonna, and Wayne. Much love to the Arnolds and Dalys. I'm lucky to come from an extended family of readers and writers—thank you all, especially Grandpa Bill, who planted the seed.

Matt Kirkpatrick. For all time.

ABOUT THE AUTHOR

Susan McCarty's stories and essays have appeared in *The Iowa Review, Utne Reader, The Collagist, Conjunctions, Indiana Review, Willow Springs*, and other journals. Once upon a time, she was an assistant editor at Penguin and Avalon Books. More recently, she's been an administrative fellow for FC2, an artist-in-residence at VCCA, and a Steffensen-Cannon scholar. She has an MFA from Vermont College and a PhD from the University of Utah. She teaches creative writing at Salisbury University.